HE SAID SHE SAID

tom
&
alice

Shannon Layne

EPIC
Press

Tom & Alice
He Said She Said: Book #5

Written by Shannon Layne

Copyright © 2016 by Abdo Consulting Group, Inc.

Published by EPIC Press™
PO Box 398166
Minneapolis, MN 55439

Cover design and illustration by Candice Keimig
Edited by Marianna Baer

LIBRARY OF CONGRESS CATALOGING-IN-PUBLICATION DATA

Layne, Shannon.
Tom & Alice / Shannon Layne.
p. cm. — (He said, she said)
Summary: When Alice gets assigned to work with Tom on a summer project, they
both think it will be a total waste of time. But Tom finds himself drawn to Alice's
fiery and bold nature, while Alice won't admit the feelings she's developing for Tom,
not even to herself.
ISBN 978-1-68076-040-8 (hardcover)
1. Summer romance—Fiction. 2. Interpersonal relations—Fiction. 3. High school
students—Fiction. 4. Young adult fiction. I. Title.
[Fic]—dc23
2015932728

EPICPRESS.COM

I want a trouble-maker for a lover,
Blood spiller, blood drinker, a heart of flame,
Who quarrels with the sky and fights with fate,
Who burns like fire on the rushing sea.

– Rumi

alice

I taught myself to read by the time I was three years old. Everyone always says they don't have any memories from that early, but I do. I remember the bookshelf in my room, with the crooked middle shelf and the pink paint. I would sit there for hours on the floor flipping through the pages of *Goodnight Moon* and *Where the Wild Things Are*. My mom had read them all to me as I'd followed each word with my finger, so when she stopped reading to me, I just started reading to myself. I remember the way the words bounced off the corners of my room, echoing inside the small space. I remember that the scratchy blanket on my bed was never warm enough, and I remember wearing the same sweater for so long that one of the arms almost completely unraveled. It wasn't that we couldn't get new things, I don't think, but just that no one noticed I needed them. I remember when the house was full of noise, and light, but then that memory faded, and was replaced by a quiet that never seemed to end. What I remember most was carrying my favorite book to my mom: *The Very Hungry Caterpillar*. My feet pitter-pattered on the floor over to where she was sitting at the kitchen table. I was tired of reading to myself; I wanted to hear the voice I loved most. She was curled up, her legs drawn to her chin on the wooden seat. I reached up on my toes.

"Mommy, will you read to me?" I asked.

"Not now, Alice," she said, and I remember the way the sound of her words blended together. I reached up anyway, setting the book down on the table, but the edge was too high and I knocked over the glass sitting in front of her. I remember the way her breath hissed out from between her teeth like a snake's, and the way her nails dug into the wood of the table. I remember the way I quailed beneath her icy stare, and the way she didn't move a muscle. What I didn't know then was bourbon soaked the cover of my book, destroying it page by page.

tom

It's not something I think about often, not anymore. For a while, after the accident, I couldn't even stand to be near a freeway. My dad got used to taking backroads and side streets. We were ten minutes late to everything because I would hyperventilate if the car went above forty-five miles an hour. It took me forever to learn to drive, to overcome the way my hands would start shaking at the sound of the engine, but I did. I learned to stay calm behind the wheel, to know that a car on the opposite side of the road wasn't something to be afraid of. I don't feel that pit of emptiness in my stomach all the time.

For a long time, I thought it was my fault. I had

been arguing with her when it happened, over something so stupid I don't even remember what it was. A part of me still thinks that if I hadn't been distracting her, she might still be alive. But rationally, I know that's not true. Rationally, I know there was nothing I could have done to prevent that truck from crashing into us head-on. I know it wasn't her fault, and it wasn't mine—it was his. It was the man behind the wheel who decided to drive with a blood-alcohol content of .21 percent.

My dad followed the story of his trial obsessively, picking up every detail he could, but I wanted nothing to do with it. I wanted to forget. And after a while, I succeeded. I didn't wake up screaming anymore or break into a cold sweat when I heard the click of my seatbelt locking into place. Only on the bad days do I remember the way her leg was twisted the wrong way, how there was so much blood her face wasn't recognizable even to me. Things like that are better forgotten. But there are also some things you can't forget no matter how hard you try.

CHAPTER 1
tom

"If anyone is interested, just let me know. I'll leave a few flyers on the desk and you can email or call me if you decide you'd like to apply for the internship."

As I wrap up my speech, I take a final glance around the room of high school seniors, all my age. Half of them are either asleep on their desks or chatting with their neighbors and the other half are staring at me with mixtures of boredom and disgust. I work part-time at the National Museum for American History and we need interns. Summer is the busiest time of year for the museum and my boss asked me to put up flyers and talk in some of my classes to get people interested. I remember how excited I was to come in as a volunteer, how enthralled I was that I got to spend my time someplace like the museum. But as I take a last survey of the room, I doubt that anyone here is going to want to intern or volunteer at a museum during odd hours for no pay. I set the flyers down on the edge of Mrs. Bronstein's desk as a face in the crowd catches my eye. Her hair is streaked with blue and pink and hangs in heavy layers around her face, but her eyes bite into mine with a clarity that catches my attention. In this crowd of heavy eyelids and slow minds, hers are bright, incredibly focused. She breaks contact before I do, turning her gaze back to the desk. She taps her fingers on the old wood and I can see how short her nails are. I snap back into reality and open the door to leave, turning away as though nothing has happened. And nothing did, really. I set off down the hallway, trying to shake off the sudden pounding of blood in my veins.

CHAPTER 2
alice

"**M**iss Bailey? Miss Bailey, did you hear me?"
Of course I heard you, you worthless oxygen vacuum.

"Alice?"

"Jesus Christ, Mr. Henry. I heard you. Just give me a second to get this straight."

He is silent, leaning back in his tall leather chair in the office I've come to know far too well in the past three years. He's used to my displays of temper and my sarcasm. And I've come to hate Mr. Henry and his patchy grey mustache more than the stupid wooden chair he always makes me sit in that's better fit for a POW camp than a vice principal's office. I guess making people uncomfortable is kind of the point, but that doesn't mean I appreciate it.

"Your grades aren't good enough to keep you afloat at this point," Mr. Henry continues despite my silence. "Barely. Especially History, by far your worst class. You're failing, if I remember correctly."

I roll my eyes, but hearing it said out loud stings. I could ace that class in my sleep if I wanted to.

"I should really just make you repeat your senior year over again," Mr. Henry continues. "You've missed too many days in addition to the issue of your grades."

"I'm not staying here another year," I snap.

"I don't know what you want me to tell you, Alice. You've been warned multiple times—your mother has been notified as well."

She won't notice. Or she won't remember.

I bite my lip, my chin in my hand. I get so many envelopes from the school that I throw them all out without even opening them at this point. I don't give a shit about my grades, but I have to graduate. I can't bring myself to not even graduate from this shithole. I wasted four years here. I'm getting a goddamn diploma.

"There has to be something," I say quietly, staring at Mr. Henry. He leans forward to straighten the nameplate sitting on his desk. I hate his hesitation and the fact that he has the power to tell me I can't graduate.

"Alice, you have an IQ of one hundred and forty-four. You're too smart to be barely passing and skipping three days of school a week."

I bare my teeth.

"I want that taken out of my file, do you hear me?" I hiss. "Take it out. That test was taken a long time ago."

Mr. Henry just sighs.

"I'm at my wits end here. I don't want to prohibit you from receiving your diploma, but my hands are tied."

I never beg, but I am close to it.

"There has to be something," I repeat. "What about summer school?"

"Even that wouldn't give you enough credits."

There has to be something else. History is my worst class; I know that already. It's not the subject itself—I actually enjoy history and I know a lot about it. It's Mr. Lionell. He's even worse than Mr. Henry. He's this old man who's shriveled up like a dried lima bean. He has these shifty black eyes that dart around like a goldfish in a bowl and he called me up to the board three times in the first two weeks of his class. The last time, he stood right behind me so close I could feel his hot breath on the nape of my neck. The buttons of his shirt were starting to press into my back when I turned around and walked straight out of the classroom and didn't look back. Since then, I go as few times a week as I possibly can.

"What about something besides credits," I say slowly. "What about a special project?"

Mr. Henry looks dubious, but if conventional methods aren't going to get me my diploma, I'm going to have to try something else.

"My grades have always been good enough to get me to graduate," I say. "It's just this past semester that they've dropped so low. History is my worst—let me do something related to history that can satisfy the grade requirement and let me graduate."

"Is there a project you have in mind?"

The dark-haired boy comes to my mind in a flash. Where had he said he worked?

"The National Museum of American History," I answer.

Mr. Henry frowns, but I can tell I've got his attention.

"I'm not sure I can allow you that kind of leeway in this situation, Alice."

"But they need interns," I protest. "For a summer internship. It's perfect—I can learn everything there is to know about American history in there. And I'll get hands-on experience and not be stuck in some stupid classroom."

I bite my tongue as Mr. Henry studies me over the edge of his silver glasses, folding his hands on the desk.

"You're smart enough to achieve any grade you choose," he muses, almost to himself. "That much is obvious. But you need to learn self-discipline and responsibility."

I resist the urge to roll my eyes at him when I'm still trying to win him over.

"I have to know you're serious about this, Alice," he says. "This will be a serious commitment that you make."

"I know," I say quietly, meeting his eyes. "I understand."

He stares at me another long moment and my nails dig into my palms as I wait for his answer.

"Alright," he says slowly, and my stomach flutters. "I'll accept this internship with the museum, providing you can secure it—if you give me at least one hundred and thirty hours performed in no more than two months' time."

"What?" I say, doing the math in my head. "I'll barely have time for anything else."

At his glower, I shut up. I need to graduate: that's more important than sitting on my couch or getting high with my friends. Not that it doesn't still rankle a little, but a girl's gotta have a little perspective.

"That's the deal," says Mr. Henry. "School ends in another week. I'll need confirmation from the museum once your schedule has been decided, and I'll be organizing weekly check-ins with your supervisor."

That safely removes any chance I had of skipping out on this, but I nod. I'm not in a position to bargain.

"And I want you organizing this, Alice. I'm not going to pull any strings to make this happen. Once you set it up, get me your supervisor's information and I'll confirm with them."

"Yeah, yeah, I get it. I won't skip out on this. There's no way I'm wasting any more time in this shithole."

"Language, Ms. Bailey," sighs Mr. Henry, but it's a half-hearted reprimand.

After my meeting with Mr. Henry, the hallways of Jamestown High School are deserted. My footsteps on the concrete echo eerily in the hallways. Everyone else has gone home. I run a hand through my hair and head toward Mrs. Bronstein's room, hoping she's still there. I need to grab one of those flyers with the dark-haired boy's information. Did he ever say what his name was? Either way, I don't remember, but we're about to know each other a lot better before the summer is over. I run over the numbers in my head again, and start to gnaw one of my nails. One hundred and thirty hours of my life, down the drain. Great. That's just fucking great.

CHAPTER 3
tom

There are muskets and bullet casings on the third floor, Confederate and Union uniforms on the second. The museum has original messages and letters sent by William T. Sherman and Robert E. Lee. There is an entire floor dedicated only to American presidents, starting with the great General Washington. A letter that Thomas Paine sent two weeks before the American Revolution began is in a glass case that I pass every day. There is a section dedicated to the 1949 Gold Rush, complete with an old pair of overalls and a mining pick. There are Old West exhibits, when America was young and untamed and men rode out on horseback to explore her boundaries, and Native American collections honoring the first people known to the land. My mom was a history professor at the University of Virginia, and a lot of the artifacts here revolve around topics she would teach in her courses. I spent so many days at the museum with her, walking around, floor by floor, our footsteps hushed by the dark velvet carpet. I think the Lincoln section was her favorite. She used to stay there reading the signs on his exhibit over and over. When she died, I started volunteering here and eventually was given a formal internship. Now that I'm about to graduate, I applied for a job. They can give me part time to start, and I'm pretty happy with that. It's not like I have a lot to do in my spare time anyway. My dad is great, but he stays locked up in his study a lot, or he's at the office. He's a research physicist, and the company he works for has him working on some sort of crazy project right now. I can't really pretend to know anything about it, except that it takes up enough time that I'm only likely to see him for a few hours a day.

I'm about to head home from the museum now

and I'm already thinking of what food we have left in the house. Hopefully my dad hasn't tried to make anything. Last time he tried to make spaghetti he set his sleeve on fire and splattered sauce all over the ceiling when he tried to put it out. I'm gathering my car keys from my new desk when my boss walks in.

"Are you all settled?" he asks. "Any more questions?"

"I don't think so," I answer. We've just finished going over my new responsibilities as a Promotional Assistant. I handle our guided tours, occasionally leading one myself, and I help out with media and advertisement for the museum. It's not a whole lot different from what I was doing before as an intern, but now I'll be overseeing any volunteers or interns the museum takes on myself. Oh, and I get my own office. It's pretty small, nothing special, but it's bigger than the closet I worked out of as an intern. There's enough space for a desk with my computer and another table by the wall. It's private, situated back into a corner hallway, but I don't mind.

"Sounds great. We'll see you Monday," says my

boss, and he shuts the door behind him. I grab my jacket and phone and start to head out. I've only got a few more days of school and then I'll be back here again. My phone starts to buzz just as I shut the door of my car and I answer it without a thought, thinking it's my dad.

"Hello?"

"Hi. This is Tom, right?"

The voice is female, low and sultry and somehow annoyed.

"Speaking." Who is this? I rack my brain—am I supposed to be taking a call from someone today? But I can't think of anything.

"This is Alice," says the voice. "I'm in a few of your classes. You spoke in my history class the other day. I'm calling about the internship."

An image flashes in my mind: the girl with the hair falling into her face, those clear eyes. I can still feel them, like they burned their way into my skin. I wonder if she's serious or just messing with me. She didn't exactly look like the kind of girl who'd be interested in something like this.

"Seriously?" I ask, and I hear her huff of breath.

"Yeah, seriously. Look, I get why you'd be skeptical. But it's kind of an emergency situation."

"What do you mean?"

There is a brief pause, as though she's considering her words before she answers.

"I can't graduate without the internship. I'm failing my history class and I need this gig to make up for it."

"How will this make up for the fact that you're failing a class?"

"I worked out a deal with Mr. Henry. A certain number of hours of work at the museum, and he'll let me graduate. So just do me a favor and let me have this job, okay? We both know it's not a lot of real work. It'll be easy, and I need it. Does that work for you?"

Her tone irritates me, as though she thinks she'll automatically get the job because she's somehow entitled to it. I sit in the front seat of my car, debating inside my head. Now that I'm in charge of the interns and volunteers the museum takes on, I need to make sure I choose people who are committed, and the last thing I need is some high school dropout who bails after a week of work.

"I don't know," I hedge. "I don't know that this is the kind of thing that would work best for someone like you."

There is another beat of silence.

"Someone like me?" she parrots. "What the fuck is that supposed to mean?"

"It just means that I need someone who's going to show up everyday ready to work. Not someone on the edge of dropping out of high school without the drive to pass a senior history class."

It sounds harsh as soon as the words leave my mouth, but her attitude is grating on me. I don't have to give her this position—a position she couldn't care less about—just because she might not graduate. How hard is it to pass a class anyway?

"You're an asshole," she hisses at me. "Don't act like you know me. You have no idea."

"I also can't have a intern who uses language like that."

To my surprise, she starts laughing.

"You are the most self-righteous person I've talked to in my life," she says. "You think you're better than me because—what? I'm failing a class and you're not? You already think you have me pegged, don't you? Stupid, flaky weirdo who doesn't deserve a chance to fix something she's messed up. Well, fuck you, Tom, and fuck this stupid job. And fuck your snotty higher-than-thou attitude."

There is a click and the line goes dead. I drop my phone and brace my hands on the wheel of my car. What just happened?

CHAPTER 4
alice

That snobby bastard. I am still fuming as I click End and throw my phone onto my bed. The old floorboards creak under my feet as I pace to my closet, to the bed, and back again. I need a cigarette. But more than that, I need this job. There are only a few days of school left and I need this thing to be lined up by then or Mr. Henry is never going to let me graduate. Dammit, dammit—why did I have to lose my temper like that? He was an ass, but if I'd kept it under control he might have given in. I gnaw on my fingernails, one after the other. I'm alone until my mom gets off of work, and I'm not sure when that will be. She works as a nurse so her shifts are odd hours a lot of the time.

I trip over the braided rug on my floor and curse. My room is at the very back of the house, overlooking the forest and the banks of the James River. The house has been in my family for generations: during the Civil War it was used as a meeting place and base for the Confederate army. My great-great-great-grandfather was a general and the house belonged to his family. There's a portrait of him somewhere in the attic, I think, and the house is full of antiques. It's strange sometimes to see the Queen Anne table we have in the kitchen next to the new refrigerator. God knows my mom doesn't make a lot of money, but somehow we always manage to get by. She has a trust fund from her grandfather and I guess there was more than enough in there to keep us afloat even during the bad times when I was little, when most days she didn't get up off the couch and the bottle didn't leave her hand. She's better now. She makes it to her shifts at the hospital at least.

The house is so big that most of it goes unused now. There are rooms that I know my mom hasn't gone into for years. A lot are just distant memories now—I'll remember a color of paint or a piece of furniture in a room that hasn't been used in years, but not much else. I can get in if I really want to. The master key is in my mom's room, in the drawer of her nightstand, under the picture of her and my father. That's where she hides everything. But the empty rooms hold little appeal for me. Everything I need is already here. But that doesn't mean I don't think of those forgotten places and their dusty corners, the floors desperately in need of sweeping.

The entire house needs a new coat of paint, for that matter, and there must be holes in the roof because there's a spot in the parlor where rain always drips in during the winter. But I love this house. Technically, it belongs to my mother, but she just lives in it. I know every inch of it as well as my own skin, every hidden hallway and creaky stair. It's mine. But in this moment, it's a prison. All I can think about is stupid Tom Sullivan. I have to have this job. There is no way Mr. Henry is going to negotiate with me on some other project—it was hard enough to get him to agree to this. I sit on the edge of my bed and pull my quilt onto my lap, but I just start working it with my fingers. I toss it aside, grab my phone and start looking up the number for the museum. I am not letting this go without a fight. If that's what Mr. Snobby Asshole thinks, he has another thing coming.

CHAPTER 5

alice

It was much easier than I thought it would be to find his place after that guy from the museum let me have his address. I can be very persuasive—when I'm not losing my cool, that is. I won't make that mistake with Tom Sullivan again.

I park my Jeep across the street from his apartment. It's in the middle of the city, closer to our high school than my big house on the river, but I don't envy his proximity. I'd take my house with the creaky boards and huge windows over this cramped cement cage any day. Just being this close to so many people makes me shudder. I slam the door to my Jeep and brace against the gust of wind that blows in my face. It's been hot and humid all day, and when I look up I see the dark clouds gathering in the sky. The incoming thunderstorm makes me smile darkly. I like it when the weather matches my mood.

I bang on the door, three sharp raps. There is a moment of silence, and then I hear a rustle from inside. I knock again, harder, and the door flies open.

He is taller than I remember from class. I don't know him well at all—I would say I recognize him from some of my classes and passing him in the hallway, but that's it. I tilt my head back so I can see him more clearly. He has dark hair that's falling into his face, like he runs his hands through it unconsciously and messes it up. His eyes are a sharp green, sharper than usual at the moment, perhaps, since he also looks pretty angry.

"Tom Sullivan?" I ask sweetly, and thunder rumbles. "Can I come in?"

Without waiting for an answer, I breeze past him through the open door. He fumbles for a moment and then recovers, shutting the door behind us. The living room is so neat that the edges of the perfectly arranged items hurt my eyes. The couch is a functional brown, the coffee table made out of glass so clear it's like it's not there. The ceilings are high, the floor carpet, but I can see the sheen of hardwood in the dining room. I finish my perusal and turn back to Tom, who is still staring at me like I'm the Ghost of Christmas Past about to rip his heart out. His feet shift on the carpet, creating a rustle in the silence. He cracks first.

"What are you doing here?"

I fist my hands on my hips, ready for a fight.

"I came to convince you to let me have the internship."

"You stalked me, thinking that would improve your chances?"

"I did not stalk you. And for the record, I would be a much better receptionist than the guy who gave a stranger your address."

Tom grits his teeth and a muscle flexes in his jaw.

"I told you what I thought of your inquiry—no,

your demand for the job," he says. His voice is cold. "My response isn't going to change because you come here and throw a tantrum."

"This isn't a tantrum." And it's true; I'm calm now, much more so than I was after our phone call. I fold my arms. "I'm sorry I was rude on the phone. And I'm sorry I acted like the internship isn't important when it obviously means a lot to you. I spoke rashly."

Now he looks like I just slapped him over the head with a red-hot poker. I resist the urge to roll my eyes. He seems totally incapable of keeping up with me.

"I'm sorry, too."

Well, well, well. Now I'm surprised. I arch an eyebrow at him and he shrugs before giving me his first real smile, slow and a little shy.

"Really?" I ask, and he laughs.

"Yeah. You might have been rude, but so was I."

"Thanks for admitting that."

"I'd be scared not to. You drove to my house. No, you found my address and then drove to my house. I'm a little freaked out by that, but I'm also impressed."

I slide my palms down the front of my jeans. I'll take that.

"So, can I have it? The internship? Your flyer said anyone would be considered—no prerequisites except to be eighteen."

He stares at me, right at me.

"You can trust me to take it seriously," I say quietly. "I need it to graduate—that's a big reason behind it, I won't lie about that. But I understand that it's a serious thing to you. And I respect that, honestly. I really do."

"I'm assuming you'd be coming in for a limited amount of time?" says Tom, and my stomach leaps.

"Yeah. Just until I finish the hours Mr. Henry set for me."

He runs a hand through his hair and my stomach takes another unexpected twist that I don't have time to analyze.

"I'll be on time. I'll be there every day, if that's what you want. I'll dust artifacts or polish Abe

Lincoln's boots or do whatever it is that an intern does."

"You'll probably end up doing both of those things over the course of the summer, but we don't let newbies touch the boots. Those are reserved for veteran employees."

I blink at him. I think he's joking but I'm afraid to laugh in case he's being serious. He studies me for another moment, a smile quirking up the edge of his mouth.

"Fine. You can have the position."

I forget the whole play-it-cool thing I have going on and start jumping up and down.

"Seriously?! Seriously, I can have it?"

"Yes, yes you can. Calm down, you're going to get my dad out here."

"Sorry."

I plant both feet on the ground but I'm still too excited to stand still. I run a hand through my hair again and that seems to catch his attention.

"Oh, yeah. There are a few things we need to go over before this is official."

"Like what?"

"Just some paperwork you'll need to fill out. And then we'll go over what your job will be like—dress code, things like that."

"Dress code?"

"It's a museum, Alice. Not a rave."

He is such a grandpa. I sigh, already mentally scanning my wardrobe. I plop down on the couch, and he follows me after a beat of hesitation. I don't have a lot in the way of business casual, but my mom and I are nearly the same size, and she's got enough clothes to start her own runway show. She was a secretary before she went back to school for nursing and before I was born. And God knows she never throws anything away. I'll find something in that closet.

"There's something else."

"What?"

He looks uncomfortable. He's a few inches away from me but he smells good somehow, like books and laundry.

"Spit it out, Tom," I say impatiently.

"It's your hair," he sighs. And then, to my shock, he bursts out laughing. "That sounded really weird, but yeah, it's your hair. And that ring in your lip."

"What's wrong with my hair? Or my face, for that matter?"

"There's nothing wrong with either," he says, and his face is so earnest I bite back a smile. "Really, this isn't my decision. But the museum has a strict policy."

I wave my hands in the air irritably.

"I'll take out the piercing," I acquiesce. "And if my goddamn hair can't be blue and pink, then fine. Fine. I'll dye it back to my natural color."

"Just as long as it's one color."

"This is a weird conversation."

"I know. But I'm your boss. Well, kind of."

"You're my supervisor."

He nods and smiles at me and I stand up with a sigh.

"Well, I better go. Sorry for invading your privacy again and all that."

"It's alright," he says. He heads toward the door

and opens it for me, but it doesn't feel like he's rushing me out. Just that he's trying to be polite.

"You can start Friday," he says. "Just head over to the museum after school is out and we'll get everything straightened out."

"Will I be there long on Friday?"

"I don't think so. A bit of paperwork and introductory stuff to get you started and that should be all."

"Okay. Good."

"Why?"

"Well, it's the last day of school. There are a lot of after-school activities going on."

He looks at me quizzically, the door still open an inch. Warm air blows in, but it smells like rain.

"I'll tell you more about it on Friday," I hedge. Somehow I don't think telling him I want to go out and party Friday night will look good now that he's just told me I can have the job.

"Okay," he says, shrugging it off. "I'll see you Friday then."

I nod and edge past him into the doorway. The

wind blows the door back a couple feet before Tom stops it; the storm is coming.

"Are you okay to drive home in this?" Tom asks.

"Yeah. I can handle this."

He glances across the street at my Jeep and raises his eyebrows.

"Is that your car?"

"Yeah. Why?"

"No reason," he mutters, and I shrug and start to head out the door but the wind blows me straight backwards and I stumble into his arms. Briefly, I'm up against his chest, pressed against his button-up flannel shirt and his heartbeat, and then he puts his hands on my shoulders and steadies me.

"Sorry," I say. I'm a little flustered, and I'm never flustered.

"No problem," says Tom, and he seems so calm it annoys me for some reason.

"See you Friday," I say, and I stomp off toward my car with a little more force this time, fighting the efforts of the wind to blow me back into his arms. I open the door and slam it behind me, shivering a little as I start the engine. He is still standing in the doorway as I pull into the street, and I'm not sure if the chill that runs through me is from the cold or remembering the way it felt to have his arms wrapped around me.

CHAPTER 6

tom

I shut the front door behind me with a small click and turn back to my living room. It seems smaller now that she's not here. I head back toward the couch and sit down again.

I can't believe she came here. I can't believe I said I'd take her on as an intern. I think back to her striped blue and pink hair, the lip ring, and groan inwardly. All I can do at this point is pray she listens to me and deals with those before Friday, or my boss is going to have a heart attack when she walks into the office.

If she's wearing those tight jeans again, I might have a heart attack myself.

As soon as the thought enters my mind, I shut it back down again. No way. She's going to be my employee. She's also really, really not my type. Her hair looks like cotton candy, for God's sake. I hear footsteps and my dad shuffles in, blinking at the light like a bat. His hair is sticking straight up in the back, as though he's been running his hands through it. Just like me.

"Is there someone here?" he asks, peering at me through his glasses. His sweater is checkered red and black, untucked on one side.

"No," I sigh, standing up again. Might as well get dinner ready. I head toward the kitchen and he follows. "Someone was, for a minute, but she's gone now."

"She?"

"Yeah. A girl from school."

At my dad's raised eyebrows I quickly set down the jar of spaghetti sauce I've just grabbed from the cupboard and raise my hands.

"Not like that," I say. "She's going to be my new intern for the museum."

"Oh," he says. He saunters over to grab a pan from a different cupboard but I know the wheels are turning in his mind. "It sounded like there was a lot of yelling for it to just have been a new museum intern."

"I'm sorry if we were loud. I didn't mean to disturb you."

"It's fine, Tom. I wasn't bothered by the noise. It was nice, actually."

I nod and pour the pasta in to boil. I know what he means. The apartment is always so quiet with just my dad and me. We used to live in a house further from the city, but when my mom died the extra space just became unnecessary. I used to walk in on my dad standing in the closet holding something of hers in his hands—a shirt, a sweater. I think it was just too much for him to stay in the house where everything reminded him of her. And the apartment is fine for just the two of us. I guess I didn't realize how quiet it was until today.

My dad starts slicing sausage for the pasta sauce and I watch him out of the corner of my eye until he sets the knife down. He nearly cut his finger off a couple of years ago slicing eggplant and since then it makes me nervous to see him with a sharp utensil. I drain the spaghetti noodles and toss them with the sauce while my dad puts garlic bread in the oven and then sets it on the table when the timer beeps.

It's a well-coordinated routine—we've had a lot of practice. My dad sets out glasses of milk and I hand him a plate before digging in. When we're both seated at the round table he pushes his glasses back and peers at me again as though I'm one of his samples he's studying.

"You're graduating on Saturday," he says, and I nod at him in between bites.

"That's right."

"That's a big accomplishment."

I shrug. "I guess."

"It is. And speaking at graduation is an achievement as well. Second in your class."

I gulp down milk. It makes me feel weird to be congratulated on that.

"I wish you'd change your mind about college."

"We've talked about this."

"I know we have."

"I'm going. Of course I'm going. I'm just not going right after I graduate. I want to work for a while."

My dad frowns, a line appearing between his eyebrows. This is a sore point with us, but not one I'm willing to back down from.

"You got some good offers."

"Because you submitted the applications."

"Tom, I'm just saying. You could go to any one of the places that accepted you."

I rub a hand over my face.

"Just consider it, alright?"

"I will, Dad. I promise I will."

We finish in silence and I grab his empty plate to take to the sink. He pats my shoulder and walks down the hallway toward his study. I hear the door shut and I rub my forehead with one hand.

My mom would be furious if she knew I was planning on taking a year off before I went to college. She was the one who bought me my first set of vintage mysteries and laughed when I read them all in a week. She used to sit next to me, each of us with a Sudoku book in our hands, playing game after game for hours. She sat and talked about my assignments with me even though I never needed help, just because she cared about what I was learning. School has always been easy for me and I do want to go to college. Of course I do. I want it more than anything. Just not yet.

My phone buzzes in the living room and I'm walking toward the noise when the first flash of lightning illuminates the window, followed by a roll of thunder.

"Looks like a summer storm," my dad calls from his study. "That thunder sounds like it means business."

"The rain is coming down now," I answer. My dad emerges from his work and comes to stand beside me in the living room, watching the warm rain come down in sheets.

"I could put a movie on," he says suddenly. He

looks so awkward standing there in his sweater, tall and bony and hunched over a little, as though he's still squinting at tiny printed text. We used to do that as a family when there were thunderstorms, and even though it's been years since my mom has been gone, I can't remember the last time we watched a movie together.

"Sure," I say. "Yeah, go ahead and pick one out. I'm good with whatever. Want popcorn?"

He nods, and five minutes later, we're on the couch with the TV on. The movie rolls on and then I remember my phone. I snag it from the side table and there's a text from a number I don't recognize.

What time do I have to be there Friday? Just wondering if I have time to make an apt. w/ a stylist that day. Since a certain dictator thinks he can tell me what color my hair should be.

I grin, thinking again of the way she stood in my house with her hands on her hips and made me feel like she was the one in charge. Those eyes of hers were sharp enough to shred me to pieces.

I settle into my chair and start texting her back. I think that girl made me laugh more in ten minutes than I have in a year.

The next few days pass even more slowly than usual as the last days of school drag on.

Sometimes I pass Alice in the hallway and she nods at me or says hi, which surprises me. I can't keep up with her: one minute she's so mad at me she's driving to my house to tell me off, and the next, she's waving at me with a smile on her face. It was more of a sneer if I'm being honest, but close enough.

When the last bell finally rings, I shoulder my backpack and head straight out for the parking lot, nodding goodbye to a few friends of mine as I go. I'm really more interested in getting to the museum and starting on some work that's been sitting there since I left a few days before.

The bright colors of Alice's hair catch my eye in the parking lot. She's talking to a group of people near the black Jeep I recognize from her visit to my place. I unlock my Tacoma and I think she glances toward me but I can't be sure. I pull out and head to work, shutting out the sounds of last-day-of-school revelry behind me.

CHAPTER 7
alice

I watch him pull out of the school parking lot while I head to my Jeep, calling goodbyes as I go. I'm not at all sad for school to be over. Plus, there is going to be a huge party tonight at my friend Noah's house. His parents are out of town and his older brother already got him a keg. But for now, I need to get to the salon and make Tom Sullivan eat his words. I snagged my mom's emergency credit card and I'm not skimping on anything for my makeover. Not only am I going to look the part, I'm going to make it look like I deserve it.

It takes Stacey nearly two hours to do my hair and all she's doing is dyeing it back to its natural color. I suppose me trying to fix my makeup in her mirror at the same time wasn't ideal for her. I wiped off my typical dark eyeliner and added mascara and a touch of shimmer eye shadow while Stacey styles my hair until it falls in soft waves down my back. She twists it into a chignon at the back of my neck and we study my reflection in the mirror once we're finished.

"How do I look?" I ask.

"Like a combination of a CEO and a sort of high-class escort."

"Perfect."

CHAPTER 8
tom

I'm just finishing the final touches on a memo when I hear the click of heels coming from the foyer. My desk is past the security area around the left corner toward the front doors, so I'm hidden from view but close enough to hear people enter the building. I just pressed my desk into the corner of the room by the window and I think I've finally found space for everything. I refocus my attention back to the memo I'm writing for my boss when I hear a light tap on my door. I spin around in my chair and my pulse spikes.

She is wearing a black skirt, tight and fitted, but so long it comes to her knees. Her legs are long and slim, nails still bitten short but painted a shiny blood-red. Then there is some sort of flowy top and a sharp black blazer with a red scarf that brings out the blush in her cheeks. Something shiny makes her lips glisten pink. Her eyes are the way I remember them from that day in the classroom, but without all the dark gunky stuff: bright and clear and a color I've never seen before. They're brown, but so light they're like liquid amber, shining in her face. I realize I've been staring at her in silence for nearly ten seconds. I need to say something. Anything. I clear my throat, searching for words appropriate for an office instead of the ones in my head.

"You, uh, changed your hair," I say, and it sounds stupid as soon as it comes out of my mouth. But it's true. Where before there were blue and pink streaks and messy pieces in her face, Alice's hair has been dyed a dark blonde and tucked back neatly.

"Yeah, well," she shrugs. "You told me I had to. And I like change."

"It looks really nice," I say lamely.

"Nice?" She raises an eyebrow, and I want to say that it's more than nice, that she looks perfect, but I just clear my throat and stand up.

"Yeah. It's fine."

"I'm glad you . . . think it's fine."

The edge of her mouth is tilted up slightly, like she's toying with me, and I guess she is. I brush it off and close my mind to the fact that she's also wearing some sort of perfume that smells like coconut. It reminds me of beaches and palm trees. But I'm not thinking about it.

"Let's get you set up," I say.

We spend the next hour going through the logistical process of getting Alice registered as an official museum intern. She needs a nametag and pass card to get through security every day, first of all. I take her through getting her picture taken and printed onto a pass and activating it. She also has to be fingerprinted for security reasons, and then there's a pile of paperwork for her to fill out.

"Why do you need to know my social security number?" she demands. "What if someone steals my identity?"

"No one is going to do that. It's just a security thing."

She mumbles something about corporate greed, still looking suspicious, and goes back to filling out the page. I suppress a grin. Something I'm learning is that, to Alice, anyone trying to tell her what to do is someone to be suspicious of. A part of me has a growing appreciation for her fierce defense of her own freedom. I wonder if it's hard for her to be here, taking orders from me.

I glance over and can see that her handwriting is surprisingly small, neat. But she presses the pen into the page so hard I'm afraid it's leaving marks on the little table I pulled up for her. She finishes the last page and slides it toward me and I add it to the pile.

"Alright," I say. "I think that's good for tonight."

"Really?"

"Yeah. You have your pass now. On Monday just come through security and I'll get you set up for your first real day."

"I don't have to work on the weekend?"

"No. I'm not here, so you can't really come in, either."

"Works for me," she says breezily. She stands up, smoothing her skirt down with both hands. "I'll see you on Monday, then?"

"Yeah. I'll be here."

She smiles at me, grabbing her bag and pass card in one big jumble as she heads for the door. She pauses and turns around and I immediately try to look as though I wasn't just staring at her butt in that skirt.

"There's a party tonight. You're not going?"

"I wasn't planning on it."

"Okay. Well, I'll be there if you end up changing your mind and want directions or something."

"Okay. I'll, uh, let you know."

She nods and heads out, letting the door fall shut

behind her. The sudden silence seems louder than the chatter of her voice. I force my attention back to my computer, pushing the lingering scent of coconut out of my mind.

CHAPTER 9
alice

As soon as I get home I strip myself out of my mom's clothes and hang them back up in her closet. She got home late last night and took a bottle of bourbon to bed with her. She did get up this morning to make me oatmeal though, even in her oldest pink bathrobe and slippers. So there's that. Then it looks like she went back to bed. She's still passed out and will be until her alarm goes off to wake her up for her next shift. I can walk in and out of her room, even flick on the light, and she doesn't even shift in her sleep. How the hell do we have anything left in this house? Why don't people just rob us blind while I'm at school?

I lean over to double-check her alarm and brush the hair back from her face. It's a dark honey-blonde, like mine. I have her small, upturned nose, the freckles on her cheeks. But her eyes are a blue so bright it hurts to look at them. My eyes are my dad's. When my parents split up my mom couldn't look me in the eyes for weeks. She would barely speak at all at first, and once she did she couldn't look at me. Her gaze would flick around me, to the wall or a chair or a painting, but never to me. I thought there was something wrong with me for a long time, until I saw the picture of my dad in her drawer. Relatives had always exclaimed when they saw me, saying I was the spitting image of my father, but I didn't really understand until I saw the picture. In the photo he is turned toward the sunlight, an arm draped around my mom's shoulders. She is laughing, head tilted toward the sky. His eyes are crinkled in a smile, the exact shade of mine. I don't know why she still keeps that stupid picture.

I turn from my mom's bed and head up the

creaking staircase, yanking the bobby pins from my chignon. Tom was pretty quiet about my makeover. He noticed, alright—stared at me for nearly a minute—but then didn't say barely a word about it. I roll a shoulder back against the tension in my neck, irritated without understanding why. I shake my hair out, letting it fall and spread across my shoulders, and feel better.

One of my friends, Sara—I wouldn't say we're really *friends,* more like occasional associates—already texted me and said she could give me a ride. In my room, I throw open the squeaking double doors of my old armoire and study the contents, opening the closet too for good measure. I pull out tight black pants and a matching top that slides across my skin, then black boots. I draw eyeliner back on, lighter than normal. I leave my hair down in loose golden waves. I've just fastened my second boot when I get a text from Sara—she's here. I take the stairs two at a time and jump off the deck before sprinting to her car, my heart thudding in my chest with excitement.

The party is already in full swing by the time we arrive, but it's secluded enough so that the cops won't get called—hopefully. I can hear music pounding as we park the car and walk toward the noise. People are swarming around the house, coming in and out like bees in a hive.

"I can't believe we're graduating," says Sara, grabbing my arm. "Graduation practice tomorrow is going to be a bitch."

"Yeah it is," I agree. It's scheduled for nine in the morning at the high school. Mr. Henry is letting me walk, although he says he won't give me my diploma until I finish my internship. I'm a little excited to wear the stupid cap and gown, even though that makes me feel like a dork. I think Tom is speaking, actually. I can't picture someone so serious and shy speaking in front of that many people. I check my phone again, but he hasn't texted me. I feel a little flash of disappointment, but before I can wonder why I care, Sara knocks on the front door and we're engulfed in the noise and chaos.

After two hours, I've said hi to at least thirty

people and also downed anywhere between three and six shots of raspberry vodka. I look down and am mildly surprised to find another in my hand, and I toss it back as the group cheers. I'm warm, floaty, and none too steady on my feet, and I feel wonderful. I understand why my mom drinks the way she does. It makes you happy and numb all at the same time. But I still wouldn't trade it for my reality. She would, though. She does every fucking day.

My phone buzzes in my back pocket and I grab for it clumsily, nearly dropping it into someone's cup in the process.

You left your scarf here. I can bring it for you on Monday.

I giggle. He's so formal about everything. I start to text back that Monday is fine when a guy walks up and slings his arm around my shoulder.

"Hey, beautiful," he says. His name is Kyle. He sits behind me in Anatomy and is always poking me or trying to get me to turn around. He's on the football team. Or is it soccer? He tugs my phone from my hand and starts pressing random buttons.

"Hey!" I protest, trying to grab it, but he just lifts his arm above his head, laughing. Drunk men are obnoxious.

"Jump a little higher, Blondie," he teases. "Wasn't your hair pink earlier?"

"Shut up," I say, snatching my phone back. Dammit. Somewhere in the scuffle he must have hit Send, because I texted Tom back a jumble of letters. I start to explain the accident when a new message appears from him on my screen. That was fast. Someone thrusts another shot glass into my hand and I tip it back without conscious thought.

Are you okay?

I resist the urge to roll my eyes. I want to respond, *Yes, Dad, I'm fine*, but I resist.

Yeah, sorry, someone had my phone. I'm good.

Another instantaneous response: *Do you have a ride home?*

I start to shove my phone back into my pocket

without responding when his name appears on my screen. Is he calling me? I walk toward the bathroom, hoping for quiet, and stumble right into the door before I find the handle.

"Hello?" I try to straighten up my hair in the mirror. Sometime over the course of the night it's gotten a little crazy.

"Alice?"

"Yeah?"

"Do you have a ride home?"

"Yeah, Tom. I'm fine. Sara is driving. Sara is totally driving."

Are the lights in here spinning, or is that just me?

"Is she sober?"

I try to focus on the question he's asking me and not the strange roll of my stomach.

"Yeah. I mean, she'll be fine."

"Is she sober or not?"

"Is it any of your business, Ociffer Nosy?" I mix up the *f*'s and *c*'s in *officer*, but whatever.

"Just answer me."

"She's had a few drinks, but she can drive. Someone will get us home, okay? Calm down." I giggle incoherently for no reason I'm aware of, and out of nowhere, my throat constricts. I heave violently into the toilet, falling to my knees as the alcohol I've consumed in the past two hours makes a reappearance. It stings the back of my throat and brings tears to my eyes as I gag. Everything is suddenly much too fuzzy, and I feel like I'm spinning in midair. I don't think I could get off the floor by myself if I wanted to. I gasp for air, wiping my mouth with the back of my wrist. I can vaguely hear Tom on the phone still, calling my name, and his voice feels like the only thing left linking me to reality. How much did I drink? The question is moot at this point—obviously too much, and the damage is done.

"Tom," I gasp, grabbing my phone from the floor and pressing it to my ear. "Come get me," I say. "Can you come get me? Please."

"Tell me where you are."

"Twelfth and Flora. The house with the . . . the house with the party."

"Hang on, Alice. I'll be there in a minute."

The line goes dead, and I slide to the floor, pressing my cheek to the cool tile.

CHAPTER 10
tom

I can hear the party before I see it. The music is up to blasting and there are lights shining out of every window. The people have spilled onto the street and there is a crowd standing by the front door, smoking. I shake my head. This party is just waiting to get busted. I'm surprised the cops aren't on the way yet. I was sitting on the couch with a mystery novel when I remembered Alice's scarf and thought I'd let her know I had it. It's a lame excuse, even in my head. I wanted to talk to her. And when she asked me to come and pick her up I knew I didn't have a choice. Her voice was muffled, slurred, and it didn't sound like anyone at the party was going to be any help.

I shoulder my way through the crowd, ignoring the smell of smoke and spilled alcohol. The inside of the house is even worse. I snag someone's arm and ask if they've seen Alice, but they're too drunk to answer me. My stomach rolls as the smell of alcohol worsens. She'll probably think I'm insane tomorrow for coming to pick her up. There are people flopped over on chairs, on the floor, others who haven't passed out are stumbling past me, laughing and tripping over the ones on the floor. No one has even noticed me walk in. I shoulder my way past a couple making out against the bathroom door and bang on it.

"We've been waiting forever," complains the guy, removing his lips from his girlfriend's long enough to inform me of the bathroom wait time. I ignore him and pound on the door again. Alice was in the bathroom when we talked, and it doesn't look like anyone here is in any shape to have moved her since then. In my chest, there is a flicker of fear.

"Alice?" I call. "Alice, open the door."

All I can hear from inside the bathroom is silence,

and I start to panic again. She's in there by herself—
what if she's not breathing? What if she choked? I
pound harder, but there's still no response. I twist
the door again and finally lean my shoulder into it
in one hard shove. It holds, but with another shove
I hear the dull click as the lock breaks and I finally
get the door open. Sure enough, she's lying on the
ground with one hand tucked under her chin and
the other arm straight out under her head. Her hair
is a tangle of gold on the floor and I bend down
but it's obvious she's breathing, just passed out. The
knot of uneasiness unravels a little in my chest. She's
okay. I nudge her shoulder and she doesn't move
an inch.

"Alice," I say, shaking her harder. "Alice, come
on."

She is completely unresponsive. For a second I
debate taking her to the emergency room, but then
her eyes flutter open.

"'M fine," she mutters, patting my cheek with
her hand. "Hi, Tom."

Then just like that she's back asleep. I breathe a

sigh of relief, resigning myself to carrying her out, knowing there's no way she's going to help me out at all at this point. I grab her phone where it's lying on the bathroom tile and tuck it into my back pocket before I slide an arm under her legs and another around her back. Her head immediately falls onto my shoulder. She snuggles closer in her sleep and I stand up, adjusting her in my arms. I push past the making-out couple still in line and head toward the front door. I get a few weird looks but nearly everyone is just too drunk to care or notice, or at least too drunk to try to stop me. I see the girl Alice said was supposed to be driving passed out in a chair and shake my head. There's no way I would have let that happen.

Alice mumbles and shifts in my arms and I move her closer, turning to get through the front door. I step free of the smoke and the smell of stale alcohol and carry her into the clear night air.

Once I've gotten her into the car I realize I don't know where to take her. Should I take her home? To my house? I don't know if taking her home will get her in trouble, but I feel like if I was a parent and my child was passed out drunk I'd want them home and safe. I dig her phone from my pocket and open her messages. She has her pass code turned off, of course. There are a few messages from Sara talking about tonight.

If you drive we can stay at my house. My mom's working the night shift and she wouldn't notice anyway.

There is another twist in my chest at the thought of no one caring whether or not Alice gets home. Well, her mom isn't my problem. At least I know now that I can take her home, although I am stumped as to where that is until I remember that I still have her paperwork from today. I reach behind me to the backseat and sift through the papers with one hand until I find one with her address on it. I turn back around in the driver's seat and reach over to fasten Alice's seatbelt. Her head drops forward and her cheek lays heavy on my hand while I struggle with the buckle, her face warm and flushed and soft against my skin. I buckle her in and gently smooth her hair back from her face and make sure her head is lying up against the headrest. Her face is perfectly calm, worry-free, like a child in the middle of a nap, and I can't help but smile despite the stunt she's pulled tonight. Was it really necessary for her to drink this much? I have no idea how much she got in her system, but it was certainly enough. I plug her address into my GPS and start the drive to her house.

CHAPTER 11
tom

As soon as we pull into Alice's winding driveway, my jaw drops for what feels like the hundredth time since I've met her. The house is a huge, rambling colonial with wide windows and shutters and a wraparound porch. It looks like the style built sometime during the Civil War era, though I'd have to do some research to know for sure. There is an outdoor balcony that seems to encompass most of the upper floor. The entire thing is set back into the forest and surrounded by huge old oak trees with the river behind it all. In the dark it's almost forbidding, the old boards surrounded by dark branches, but it fascinates me. I'd love to see it in the light. From what I can tell, it definitely looks like it could use a little work done, but all in all the outside doesn't look bad. I nearly forget about the girl beside me in my excitement about the house, and I almost blush even though she isn't awake to see me nerd out about it. I park next to Alice's Jeep and start trying to get her inside. I unbuckle her seatbelt and she immediately slumps onto my shoulder, half-falling out of the car. I scoop her up and start walking to the house when her body starts to heave.

"Shit," I hiss, trying to set her down somehow without her falling on her face. Her chest lurches forward and all I can do is support her body as it rejects everything she put into it tonight. The smell of alcohol nearly makes my eyes water, but I wait it out until her body calms again, and then continue toward the house. She still isn't talking, but as long as she's breathing and throwing up I think she'll be okay. The front door swings open at my touch and I can see that the inside of the house is as amazing as the outside. I fumble for a light switch and the foyer light flickers on, revealing high ceilings and a dusty chandelier. The walls are dark wood with intricate molding, leading me through a hallway to a massive staircase with curved railings. A lot needs to be updated and repaired, but the bare bones of the house are incredible. I carry Alice through the foyer and eye the double staircase with some trepidation. It looks steep, and Alice is tiny, but dead weight is hard to carry. I gather myself and start the long journey up, her head lolling on my shoulder.

Her room is easy to find among the rows of closed doors. It's down the long corridor and toward the back of the house. I lower Alice to her bed and settle her under the quilt. I turn to go and then turn back, torn. If I leave her now and she starts throwing up again she could die. She is curled up, a pillow held tight to her chest, and she's breathing deeply now. I tuck a lock of her hair behind her ear and she reaches up in her sleep and clutches my hand. Her fingers are long, her nails bitten to the quick. She brushes her thumb across my skin and lets go, snuggling deeper into the covers. I can't believe I'm here, in her house. It seems as though in the few days I've known Alice she's tipped my world on its axis. I'm not sure how to take it, but something is changing. Or maybe everything is changing. I grab an extra pillow and blanket from the foot of her bed and set up a space for myself on her rug. Looks like it's going to be a long night.

CHAPTER 12
alice

The first thing I'm aware of is the blinding light burning my eyes. I twist and turn but can't seem to escape it. Through the fuzziness of my head I finally reach up and fling my hand around until I find the curtain and pull it closed. In the dark again, I settle back into sleep before I realize I have no idea where I am. I sit up wildly and pillows go flying. My head reacts instantly to the assault on my senses: it starts pounding and I hiss and cover my eyes with my hands.

"Alice?" a voice from the floor calls.

Am I alive?

"Yes?" I say.

I squint toward the dark shape on the floor, and as my eyes adjust again, I realize it's a person. It's a person I know. Holy shit, it's Tom. What is Tom doing here? In painful flashes, the night starts coming back to me. I talked to him on the phone, didn't I? I asked him to come. I asked him to come and get me. I'm so embarrassed. I want to cover my head up with the comforter and disappear.

"How are you feeling?"

Oh my God, he looks perfect. A little rumpled from sleeping on the floor all night, but other than that . . . the sun is shining in his eyes and making them impossibly green, and his hair is dark and somehow perfectly messy. I try to smooth down my hair, which I can practically feel shooting into tentacles as he stands there.

"Pretty awful," I say. "How did I . . . how did you?"

"I came to get you from the party."

"Oh. Oh, wow."

"Yeah."

He shuffles a little on my rug. He's in my house.

He's here, in my house. My mind is so fuzzy that trying to think back to last night almost makes it explode, let alone try to decipher how I feel about Tom being here. I would have cleaned up a little if I'd known there would be a boy sleeping on my floor. Alright, no I wouldn't have, but I would have at least considered it.

"Thank you," I say quietly. "For picking me up. You didn't have to do that."

"You asked me to come get you."

"I know, I know I did. I just meant I didn't really expect you to come and pick me up. I appreciate it."

"You're welcome."

He's looking at me again in that quiet way he has and it's doing something to my insides. I can't believe he saw me the way I was last night. More than saw me—he picked me up. He slept on my floor.

"You took care of me?" I ask. I pull my quilt over my legs, thankful that I'm still in my clothes from last night.

"Yeah."

"How bad was it?"

He shrugs again.

"It wasn't too bad. I carried you into the house and put you to bed. You, uh, threw up a few times, but—"

"I threw up?"

"Yeah. Yeah, you did."

"Well. Well, alright then."

There is another moment of silence. There is a part of my subconscious that is rolling her eyes at me for being a drunken moron.

"Why'd you go through all that trouble for me?" I ask.

"You asked me to come get you. Once I did I couldn't just leave you alone."

"You didn't have to come and get me."

"Of course I did, Alice. You were drunk. I would never let anyone that drunk try and get home when their ride was already passed out."

Something about the way his hands clench when he says that makes me think there's more to the story than he's letting on. He changes the subject.

"I'm sorry if it feels weird that I'm here."

"It doesn't," I say. "Honestly."

And it doesn't. I might have just met him and he kind of might be my boss, but having him stand next to my bed and talk to me doesn't feel weird at all.

"I'm glad you called me," he says quietly. "When I got to the party you'd locked yourself in the bathroom. I broke the lock to get you out, and you were just lying on the floor."

Wow. He went through a lot of trouble to get me out of there. I tilt my head, studying him, and trying to ignore the pounding in my head.

"I didn't mind taking care of you at all. I'm glad you were talking to me at the time so I could get you and make sure you were safe. But you were pretty far gone. I debated taking you to the hospital."

"I'm sure it wasn't that serious," I scoff, and he looks at me so sharply it tears at me.

"Yeah, it was," he says. "It was that serious. And I know that we just met, and you barely know me, and I barely know you, but you're better than that, Alice."

I am speechless. I just stare at him, a lump lodging into my chest. I'm so used to taking care of everyone else that having someone be concerned about me is almost too much to bear. I shrug a shoulder, acting like I'm brushing off his comment.

"It was just one night," I say. "It's not a big deal. It doesn't define who I am."

He shrugs again, hands in his pockets.

"If what we do doesn't define us, then what does?"

His eyes are locked on mine again, a piercing green that delves into me. I don't know what to say.

"It's about seven now," says Tom. "So you still have time to get ready and go to graduation practice."

Oh, shit. I'd completely forgotten.

"Thank you," I say. "I totally forgot about that."

"No problem," says Tom with his first hint of a smile. "Uh, will your mom care that I slept here?"

I snort.

"No," I say. "She's working a shift right now, I think. Or she might still be sleeping off her latest hangover. Right now I can't really remember which."

Tom blinks at me, shifting awkwardly, and I realize I've embarrassed him with my honesty.

"It's fine," I say in a gentler voice. "I appreciate you staying, anyway."

Tom nods, and smiles at me with an expression I can't quite read.

"Good. I just wanted to make sure."

There is a quiet moment where I can almost hear the air rushing in and out of his lungs.

"I'm going to go home myself and shower and stuff," he finally says, "but I guess I'll see you down there? At graduation practice?"

His hands are shoved in his pockets and his hair is in his eyes, which pulls at my attention, so I answer him more slowly than I should.

"Yeah. Yeah, I'll see you later."

He grabs his jacket from the floor and leaves, closing my door quietly behind him. I sink back into my pillows. I cannot believe I was such an idiot last night. It was nice of him to take care of me. It was more than nice. I start gnawing on one of my fingernails. His words are still hanging in the air even though he's gone. I wish I had some orange juice. I wish that I'd kissed him before he left.

CHAPTER 13
alice

Graduation practice is hell. I don't have to do anything but stand up and sit down on the cues, thank God, but that activity alone is enough to make me feel like I'm going to pass out. I take another swig of the water bottle that I brought with me and squint despite my dark glasses. I managed to get in the shower and sling my wet hair up into a bun before I came here. At least I'm clean, if not feeling completely human yet. I can't stop thinking about this morning: the way Tom's eyes cut into me through the sunlight. They were a softer green than I've seen them before, like sea foam. I could barely sit up, and there he was after spending a night on the floor looking like an Abercrombie model. Every time I think of him taking care of me while I threw up, I cringe. If he had just been at the party and seen me drunk, I wouldn't have cared, but the fact that he held my hair back while I heaved is a little much for me. Why did I have to get so drunk? Why did I have to call him?

There's always been alcohol in my presence, for most of my life anyway. My mom drinks Kentucky bourbon like she's afraid they might stop making it, and we have a liquor cabinet that she keeps stocked. I drank myself sick for the first time when I was fourteen, alone in my room with a bottle of vodka. I don't even know why. Maybe because I knew I could, and no one would notice. Even if they did, they wouldn't care.

"Who's that guy up there?" mumbles Sara. I met up with her once I got here. She's just as hung over as I am. She's apologized about four times for getting drunk at the party when she was supposed to be driving, but since Tom came to get me, it doesn't matter anyway.

"Huh?"

"That guy. He's up there on the podium. Looks like he's going to give a speech today."

I peer through my glasses and realize, with a jolt in my stomach, that it's Tom.

"That's Tom," I say casually. "You know, dark hair. Kind of quiet."

"Wait. Is he the one who broke Noah's door?"

"You heard about that?"

"Everyone did! He's the one who took you from the party?"

"Yup."

"Wow. He doesn't look like the knight-in-shining-armor type, but he is pretty cute. I didn't know he was speaking."

"Neither did I," I admit. Another surge of guilt rushes through me, thinking of the time he spent with me last night. He should have been practicing his speech, not up all night with a girl too drunk to know her own name.

Tom turns on the podium to head back down to the grass and meets my eyes. He gives me a little smile and then walks back to his place in the crowd of white chairs.

"Did he just smile at you?" asks Sara. I bristle, instantly defensive, and cross my arms in front of me. My mouth flops open and closed like a fish out of water.

"No. I don't think so. I think he was looking at someone else."

She snorts.

"Nice try," is all she says.

By the time afternoon rolls around, I'm feeling halfway human again. My hair is curled in soft waves after a half hour with the curling iron, and I'm in the process of doing my makeup. My mom is working on my eye shadow.

"Stop squirming," she says, swatting at my shoulder. "You're making me smudge it."

"You're poking my eyes out."

She continues swiping pale gold shadow over my lids. I sigh, relaxing under her touch.

"Who was that nice boy who left here this

morning?" she asks. I flinch like she's just dropped an ice cube down my back.

"No one," I say. "He's a friend. How'd you notice, anyway?"

"I notice more than you think."

I choose not to answer as my mom switches out the eye shadow for mascara.

"He looked like a nice boy. His clothes were all rumpled like he'd slept on the floor."

"He did sleep on the floor."

"That's what I thought. A nice boy."

"Just a friend, Mom," I say again, but her lips hide a smile.

Mom drives me to graduation and joins the crowd walking toward the bleachers while I find my classmates. She's sitting up in the stands now, watching. I wish I were doing more than just barely graduating. I just found out that Tom is speaking at the ceremony because he's the salutatorian. I bet my mom will just love that.

She's the only family I have here. But we've

always been enough for each other, somehow. She's woven into my first memories of life, the good and the bad. They call my row forward and I stand, tripping over the edge of my stupid gown. I hand my card to the speaker and he says my name as I cross the stage.

"Alice Marjorie O'Callahan Bailey," he says, and I roll my eyes even as I throw my chin in the air and begin the walk across the stage.

My name is a nightmare. It's my mom's fault. The O'Callahan is her side of the family. The ones who passed down our house to her. They were Irish who came across the sea to seek their fortune and found it in cotton and tobacco. And now, lucky me, I get to carry on the family name.

I see my mom waving to me out of the crowd and I soften as I wave back. I step off the other side of the stage, and it's over. I have to say, it feels a little anticlimactic. And now I have a month of spending every single day at the museum to look forward to. I try to squash down the little thrill of excitement that shoots down my spine at the thought.

I can't quite get the image of a certain pair of dark green eyes out of my head.

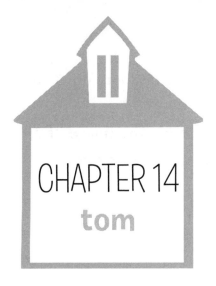

CHAPTER 14
tom

It takes me nearly twenty minutes just to find my dad after the ceremony ends. The crowds of people surround me on all sides until I finally spot his glasses in the sea of faces.

"Congratulations, son," he says, slapping me on the back. My speech was fine. Luckily, public speaking doesn't seem to affect me too much. There are worse things, I guess.

"Thanks, Dad," I say. "Did you like the Roosevelt quote?"

"Oh, I enjoyed it immensely," he says with a smile.

Then, from behind me, a voice I'm beginning

to recognize—sultry, with a sarcastic edge—says, "I just knew there would be something nerdy in there."

I turn and there's Alice, looking completely different than the girl I saw this morning. She was still lovely, unfairly so, but now she's even more than that. Her hair falls in silky waves and her eyes are tawny in the sun. She has something shimmering on her eyelids. It's distracting.

"I'm Alice," she says, extending a hand to my dad, and I instantly flush. I've been too busy ogling her to introduce them.

"Roger," my dad says politely.

"I'm a friend of your son's," says Alice. "I'm sure you heard me the other day. I was the one yelling in your apartment."

"Were you now?" says my dad, arching an eyebrow. I shrug sheepishly.

"And did you enjoy the Roosevelt reference in Tom's speech?" my dad adds.

Alice smiles. "I think I'd be stupid not to enjoy

anything that Tom wrote. Although I'm more of a literature nerd than a history nerd like him."

I raise my eyebrows. Leave it to Alice to compliment and insult me at the same time.

"Well, it was nice to meet you," she finishes. "I'm sure I'll see you again soon."

She flashes a smile at both of us and saunters off. We stare after her. I reach up and rub the back of my head.

"Is she the one you hired to work at the museum?" my dad asks.

"Yup."

"Good luck with that, son," he says, and I don't even want to ask him what he means. I can handle Alice. I can handle her.

Even as I think it, I can hear my own subconscious laughing at me.

The rest of the weekend—my first weekend as a high school graduate—drags by. I don't have to be in the museum until Monday, and I find myself twiddling my thumbs. I draw out a more concrete schedule for the things I need to go over with Alice, but I end up spending more time tracing her name in pencil than I do planning.

I pick up books and set them back down. I start projects and lose interest halfway. I can't focus on anything but the thought of seeing her again.

I'm just not sure how I went from yelling at her on the phone to spending the night in her bedroom. All I did was sleep on the floor, but the little hints of her I picked up on are locked in my mind. Now I know that she has incense on her windowsill, and coconut body spray on her dresser. She sleeps on her side and she always has to have a pillow in her arms. She snores.

I trace her name in pencil again and sit back in my chair at my kitchen table. I'm excited and afraid for Monday to come. I'm not used to this tornado of emotions that Alice brings out in me. And she's a far shot from perfect—I saw her at her worst on Friday night. But it concerned me more that she could have put herself in danger than it did that she was drinking. I came to get her because I wanted to make sure she was okay, and because on some level I knew I didn't want anyone else to be the one taking care of her.

CHAPTER 15

tom

Monday comes, and it's torture and excitement mixed into one. I'm up early, making myself a mug of coffee, and drinking it so fast it burns my tongue. I make another cup despite the fact that I don't need any more caffeine. I'm already so energized I wish I had time to do something before work to take the edge off. Like run a marathon.

"What's got you so antsy?" asks my dad, and I just shrug. He seems more cheerful than normal too, though, as he pours himself a bowl of cereal and sits down to read the paper. I grab a thermos and head out the door. I don't know what's gotten into me, but I blame it on the fact that my summer is just beginning. It's definitely related to the weather somehow.

By the time 9:25 rolls around, I'm tapping my fingers and watching my office door, more annoyed than excited. Dammit, it's her first real day. She could at least try to show up on time. I'm starting on my emails again when she finally rushes into my office, a whirlwind of clicking high heels and flying hair.

"Hi, hi, hi," she says breathlessly. "Sorry. I stopped to get coffee. Big mistake."

She walks right in and drops a Starbucks bag on my desk.

"I brought you a scone," she says, flashing me a wide smile. "One of those tiny vanilla bean ones. Okay, there were more, but I ate them."

"It's okay," I say. She's wearing black again, trim slacks and a fitted top that shows her shoulders. She has red slicked over her lips and her hair is a cloud of gold. I take several deep breaths. She's my employee. This is a mantra I must repeat. She sits down in the chair in front of my desk and nibbles at my scone, grinning at me. Her mood is always throwing me off: one minute she's sarcastic and snappy and the next she's beaming at me and bouncing out of her seat. It's fascinating.

"I'm ready," she says. "What do you have for me today?"

"A lot," I say, trying to refocus my thoughts, but they seem to scramble in her presence. "Uh, I'm going to start you working on a lot of our marketing schemes. There's a lot for people to do here—interactive activities and seminars and such—that the museum puts on and that not a lot of people are aware of. I'm going to get you started on a few projects that have been on hold regarding that stuff."

"Mhmm," she says, leaning forward. I catch a whiff of coconut and my head swims.

"Yeah. Um, then I thought you might like a tour of the museum itself. You should be familiar with the floor plan and the exhibits."

"Sounds fun," she says. Her eyes are focused on

me, almost golden in the light coming in through my window.

"It should be instructive," I say dryly, and she smirks at me. "Anyway, that's what we'll start with. If you are interested and if you can pass the necessary testing, I can also consider making you a tour guide."

"Is that a lot of work?"

"It's a fair amount of memorization."

She shrugs. "I'll think about it."

"We can look over the script later and see what you think."

She nods and I get her started on the first steps of a marketing project that I think she'd enjoy. I also give her a ton of resources about the museum itself—the exhibits, the research it funds, some fun facts about the artifacts we have on display. I might be a history nerd but I think the fact that we have Ben Franklin's homemade telescope here is pretty freaking cool. She works off the laptop that was brought in and set up for her on Friday. The little table she sits at is close enough for her scent to blow over me every time she runs her hands through her hair. I wish I could stop thinking about how good she smells. Eventually I manage to redirect my focus and answer a few of the emails waiting for me. The research department is considering opening a new exhibit, but when I was a volunteer I wasn't too involved in it. Now that I work here officially, though, I'm helping with some of the research, and brainstorming is necessary to actually contribute. I'm drawing up a memo for my boss when Alice clicks her Starbucks cup down on her desk.

"It's about noon," she says. "I'm starving. Are you hungry?"

"Uh, yeah. A little. Is it really lunchtime?"

"Looks like it. There's a deli around the corner. Want a sandwich?"

"Sure."

"What kind? I'll go get them and we can eat in here."

"Turkey and Swiss."

"Got it. Back in a flash."

And just like that, she's out the door again. I shake my head. She has more energy than I think even she can really handle. I wonder how much of it is physical and how much of it comes from her not challenging her mind. Because the more I see of Alice, the clearer it becomes that she's not stupid. Reckless and impetuous, maybe, but not stupid. Then why did she practically flunk out of high school?

"Here you go," she says, waltzing back in my door. "Turkey and Swiss. I got you a cookie, too."

"You're going to make me fat."

She snorts, her mouth already full of sandwich.

"I doubt that," she says, eyeing my body. I glance down at myself and see what I always see—myself. I wonder what that looks like to her.

"You seem to be feeling better," I say, and her face clouds.

"I am," she says, looking down at the sandwich in her hands. "But I wish there was some way I could repay you." Since that night, she's both apologized and said she feels obligated to repay me. That core of integrity is another twist for Alice; she might seem self-centered at times, but she cares about other people more than she lets on.

"It's really not a big deal."

"Why did you come get me?"

"We talked about that already."

"Not really."

"How would you have gotten home? Drove yourself? I don't think so. I just knew you were too drunk to be safe."

"Why do you care how I get home?"

I rub a hand over my face. This is an area that I really do not feel the need to delve into.

"I just do," I say quietly. "Can we leave it at that, please?"

"Okay."

She is silent for a moment, but I know she's mulling everything over in her mind. I can practically see the wheels turning.

"I've never had someone care that way before," she admits quietly, nibbling on one of her nails. "I don't mean in a weird or romantic way or anything.

I've literally just never had someone worry about how much I had to drink or how I was going to get home. It was . . . different for me. I guess that's why I keep trying to work my head around it."

I nod slowly, processing what she's saying. It still hurts a little to know that she's telling the truth. She is someone obviously used to taking care of herself. Maybe that was why it was so easy for me to do it for her. She may have needed my help that night, but Alice is definitely no princess in distress. The more I see of her, the more I'm starting to see how capable she is, but vulnerable at the same time. She's like a puzzle that just gets more complicated with every piece you put together. We eat a little longer in silence, and then Alice sets her food down.

"Can I see the tour guide script?" she asks. "I like to read while I eat."

"Sure."

I fish the packet out of one of my desk drawers and hand it to her. Then she does one of the strangest things I've ever seen. She opens the packet and starts to flip through the pages too slowly to just be scanning them and too quickly to be reading them. She just stares at a page for a few seconds and then moves to the next. After a few minutes of this she is through the twenty or so pages in the packet. She folds it closed and glances up at me.

"What?" she asks.

"Did you just read that?"

"Sort of."

"What do you mean?

"I read . . . quickly."

"How quickly?"

She just blinks at me.

"Sort of photographically quickly."

"You have a photographic memory?"

"Essentially, yes. But it's not perfect. I make mistakes sometimes."

"Which exhibit is featured on page sixteen?"

"The Revolutionary War."

"Which began in?"

"1774."

"What military leader is mentioned at the bottom of page seven?"

"George Washington. Floor Two is his exhibit."

It's my turn to blink at her. She just shrugs at me.

"How did you fail a class?" I ask quietly. Her amber eyes widen. She bites her lip.

"I hated it," she says vehemently, the words coming through her teeth. "I couldn't make myself go. And I . . . I hated the teacher."

"Yeah. He's super creepy."

She just nods, her eyebrows drawn down in a glare as though she's remembering something awful. Her cheeks flush pink, while anger surges through me at the thought of some old asshole making Alice uncomfortable. Another part of me is still trying to absorb the way her mind works. She easily could have beaten me for salutatorian, or been our valedictorian, for that matter.

"Are you done with your sandwich?" she asks. "I've been looking forward to my tour all morning."

"Sure, I'm finished. Want me to take you?"

"Yeah."

She bounces up and heads out the door. She makes me feel like I'm always a step behind, but at the same time I don't feel left out. She's pulling me in, one smile at a time, and I'm powerless to stop it.

CHAPTER 16

alice

I've never discussed my memory with anyone other than my mom. Being honest with him just felt right, I guess. I couldn't have lied to him anyway. He just sat there, silent and staring at me in that piercing way, and I felt as transparent as glass. He didn't laugh at me or call me a liar or a freak. He just finished his sandwich like it was a normal day. I can't say how much I appreciate that. Now here he is, taking me on a tour of a history museum. And I'm excited. I don't have to be afraid here or uncomfortable. There's no teacher droning on or explaining something in the least interesting way possible. I'm just listening to Tom's voice, and it's steady and smooth and sweet. A part of me that I didn't know was coiled into knots finally relaxes, and I breathe a little easier.

"Let's start at the beginning," says Tom. "The whole museum is laid out in a way that is supposed to make sense visually as well as chronologically."

I know most of this already, having just read the packet. It's all in my head, like I'm still staring at the sheets of paper and flipping through them at will. He starts talking about the presidents and I flip to my mental image of page four. He switches back to museum protocol and I find page eight. It's so entertaining, watching him do this. He knows this place inside and out, every exhibit, every corner. He walks just in front of me, not too close and not too far, as though he's led many others down the same route. And I suppose he has. I can't stop watching the way he moves his hands when he talks. The sound of our footsteps is muffled now by the thick velvet under our feet as he leads me down another hallway. The lights flick on automatically as we pass by, illuminating paintings and statues and plaques.

"We offer headphones too," he says. "And visitors can take a self-guided tour."

"Have you ever done that?" I ask.

"Done what? Taken the tour?"

"Yeah."

"No, I haven't." He frowns, his brow creasing. "I'll have to do that sometime. Just to get a feel for what the experience is like. Or I'll have you do it for me and let me know how it is."

I nod, trying to stifle my smile. He takes everything about this job so seriously.

"How did you start working here?" I ask as we turn down another hallway and start up a flight of stairs. He pauses on his way up a step.

"I just started volunteering," he said. "I did that for a couple of years."

"A couple of years?"

He nods, and that's all.

"Why did you start volunteering?"

"I love history, all history. I used to, uh, come here when I was little."

What's funny is I can totally picture him here—a

small, dark-haired child with serious eyes staring up at the paintings. He was probably just as secretive then as he is now. I tell myself to be patient. I barely know him; maybe it will take more time for him to open up.

"Here is the Lincoln exhibit," Tom continues, effectively ending that train of conversation. "A copy of the Emancipation Proclamation is printed in the marble."

I nod, lodging the piece of information in my head. Tom stops to explain more about the exhibit and I move so I'm standing exactly where his footprints dented the thick velvet of the walkway.

Before I know it, the rest of the day is up and it's time for me to go. I pack up all my stuff into my bag, not that there's a lot to take home after my first day.

"I'll see you tomorrow," says Tom.

"Yeah," I say, opening the door. I stop and turn back to face him, and he looks up from his desk. He looks like an executive, and I have no doubt he'll end up managing this entire place if that's what he decides he wants.

"Thank you for today," I say. And I mean it. I sought this job hating the fact that I had to do it, and now I've finished my first day wondering where the time went. And Tom is to thank for that. He might be a little snobby and more than a little serious, but I figure I drive him crazy too so it must even out.

"Of course," he says. He gives me his full attention when he looks at me, and it's completely intoxicating. He doesn't glance away, or look at his watch, or fidget. He just focuses entirely on me, like there's nothing I could say that he would think was insignificant. I've never had someone look at me that way before. I smile at him and shut his office door quietly before taking off down the hallway. This day might have been a good one, but nothing beats my freedom. I can't wait to go home and go up to my room and grab a book and lie in bed. I make it all the way out to the parking lot and fumble for my keys before realizing the bright lights shining in my face are those of my Jeep.

"Shit," I mutter as I open the door and stick the key into the ignition. The engine doesn't even sputter; the battery must be dead. I slam the door and put my hands on my hips. My mom is working and I can't think of anyone else to come and get me on such short notice. I think of the jumper cables my mom has been nagging me to put in my car for ages. They're still sitting in the hallway closet as far as I'm aware. Dammit. This is just perfect. I'm digging around for my AAA card and muttering to myself when I hear footsteps and Tom appears beside me.

"What are you still doing here?" he asks.

"My battery is dead," I answer, throwing my hands into the air irritably. "I was just going to call Triple A. I have jumper cables at my house but no way of getting them."

"I can take you home so you can grab them," says Tom. "If that's alright by you."

"Thank God. I can't find the stupid Triple A card anyway."

Tom chuckles and continues walking to his car. I head to the passenger's side and start to shift my bag out of the way to open the door when he walks around to my side and does it for me. I definitely appreciate the gesture, but I smirk at Tom as he walks back to his side. He acknowledges the look with a shrug and I know he probably just can't help it. He's such a gentleman. God knows no one has ever accused me of being a lady. Just the thought makes me laugh. Nevertheless, I slide into the seat as Tom starts the car.

"I live out by the river," I say, and then stop. Of course he knows how to get to my house—he took me there Friday night.

"How'd you know where I live?" I ask. "You took me home but you've never been to my house before."

"I looked it up in your paperwork that I had from the museum," he says. I notice the edges of a blush working its way up his neck. "It was the only way I could think of figuring it out."

"Yeah. I guess you couldn't really ask me, huh?"

"No, that was out of the question at the time," he says drily, and I laugh, throwing my head back against the seat. What a ridiculous couple we must have made with me thrown over his shoulder, too wasted to give him directions to my house. I wish someone had gotten a picture, while I simultaneously thank God fervently that none have surfaced.

Tom steers us through traffic and out of the congestion of the city, toward my big rambling house by the water.

"By the way," says Tom as we pull up to the house. "Your house is incredible."

"Thank you," I say with a hint of pride. "I love it."

"It looks so old. It looks like it was built in the Civil War era."

"In the 1850s, I believe. It belonged to my great-great-great-grandfather."

"Jesus. He was a plantation owner?"

"You guessed it. They used to use the property as a base for the Confederate Army."

"You're shitting me."

I burst out laughing. I've never heard Tom say

anything remotely like that. We're on the front porch now and he's staring up at the boards like they're made of solid gold.

"Nope. My great-great-great-grandpa wasn't a big Lincoln supporter, apparently."

"It doesn't sound like it," Tom agrees as we step inside.

He walks through the foyer, eyeing the parlor and the hallway that leads to the kitchen and the downstairs guest rooms. Everything is a little dusty and more than a little rundown, but I know he can see past the dust the way I do. I forgot that Tom, being the nerd he is, would recognize the house for all its former glory as soon as he stepped inside. I smile, glad he feels the same way about the old place as I do. He stops at a painting hanging up next to the staircase and I follow, stopping a stair above him.

"Is this your grandfather?" he asks.

"You mean my great-great-great-grandfather? That's him."

"All the old stuff in this house is authentic, isn't it?"

Tom's voice is hushed, as though he's in a place deserving of reverence.

"Yeah, pretty much. It all belongs to my family for the most part. The attic is full of junk, too, stuff we don't really have room for down here."

"I would love to go through your attic," says Tom, and I burst out laughing again.

"What?" he asks, grinning at me.

"Nothing. I think that's just the first time a guy has told me he really wants to go through my attic."

I am suddenly aware of how close we are. Tom is still standing one step below me, directly in front of the painting. With me on the step above him, we're nearly at eye level. He is facing me, the grin fading from his face. My hand rests on the smooth curve of the stair banister, and my fingers dig into the wood. Everything seems to go quiet; the only things I hear are Tom's breaths and the clicking of the grandfather clock in the foyer. Tom is looking at me in that way he has that takes my breath away and I can't stand it. Oh, man. *Please don't look at me like that*, I beg silently. *Don't look at me like I'm the only girl in the world because it makes me believe I am.*

His green eyes are so focused on mine, like they're pulling me down somewhere deep and dark and dangerous. He steps a half an inch closer to me, just that much, and it breaks some barrier inside me. Before what little common sense and self-control I possess can sound alarms, my arms are sliding around his neck and our eyes lock for a breathless moment as my heartbeat slows. With the thud, thud, thud of my pulse pumping in my ears, my lips brush over his so softly they might not have met at all. Someone shudders and I can't be sure if it's him or me, but it ceases to matter. His hand comes up to wrap around the nape of my neck and pull my mouth to his. His other arm snakes around my waist and pulls me flush against him and all of a sudden there is so much heat flooding through my body I think if I looked down I'd see my skin glow. His mouth is crushed to mine and he tilts his head and takes me under. My body goes limp; my mind spins. I twine my fingers in his hair as he deepens the kiss, completely lost, and he is the first one to break away.

He is breathing hard a step below me, and his eyes are like fire.

"Um," I say, and that's all I can get out. Nothing has ever come over me before like that—his touch obliterated everything else. All this time I've spent trying to alter my reality and this was so different, so much more than I ever expected. In the buzz of the afterglow, I'm higher than I've ever been in my life.

I finally refocus on Tom and I can see his breathing has slowed. How long have we been standing here? Five seconds? Five minutes?

"I'm sorry," he says.

"Why?"

"I don't know. I'm not really sorry. I don't know what I am."

"Right."

I lock my hands together. Tom looks like a scared jackrabbit, caught in the open and about to run for cover. Now that I'm calming down enough to notice, it's pretty amusing. I tilt my head and study him and for the first time his eyes dart away from mine. Me and my impulses. I've never been good at holding back when I want something.

"Well, we'd better find those jumper cables," he finally says, shoving his hands in his pockets. I'd completely forgotten that was the reason we came here in the first place.

"Sure," I say easily, brushing by him as I head downstairs again. He stiffens as I pass him and I bite my lip to keep from smiling as he follows me. I pass back through the parlor toward the hall closet and start digging through coats and old wrapping paper.

"I know they're back here somewhere," I say, panting. "Stupid cords. I can never keep track of anything."

"Is that a Queen Elizabeth?"

I twist around, a coat sleeve falling over my eyes. He's staring at a little desk covered in dust in our parlor. When I was little I would sit there and read or draw.

"I think so," I say. "But I could be wrong."

Tom just shakes his head. I find the jumper cables and disentangle myself from the closet, waving them above my head.

"All ready," I say. "Let's go."

The ride back to my car is fraught with tension, but not the awkward kind. I have my hands wound in a tangle in my lap to keep from touching him. I keep sneaking glances at him out of the corner of my eyes while he drives facing straight ahead. But I can see how hard his hands are gripping the wheel. His jaw tightens every minute or so and I cross and uncross my legs over and over. I don't know what's happening, but it's almost more than I can bear. I need to either get out of this car in the next five seconds or I'm going to lose my mind. Brakes squeal and we're back in the museum's parking lot. I leap up, gulping in the fresh air as though I've been underwater. My cheeks are flushed and my pulse is racing so quickly the beats are starting to feel connected to each other. Tom gets out too and we lock eyes for a moment as he slams the door closed. I swear the air between us crackles, and then he is getting the cables out of the backseat. A few minutes later, my car is running and it's time for me to go. "Thank you, again," I say. "I really appreciate it." "It's no problem," says Tom, tight-lipped. I chew on my lower lip, just looking at him, and then I step into my Jeep and close my door, trying to shake my awareness of his eyes on me. I hear his car start and the sound of the engine fades away. I lay my forehead down on my steering wheel and take huge, gulping breaths. I can still feel his hands on mine, the way he pulled me closer. It makes me shudder all over again. It's only been twenty minutes since it happened and it already is starting to feel like a dream.

CHAPTER 17

alice

I spend the rest of the evening locked in my room with a book, but I can't concentrate. I turn on music, which helps me relax on a normal day, but nothing is soothing the energy inside me. I pace, and I gnaw restlessly on my fingernails, and I remember. More than anything, I remember. I have a mind that fixates on things, and right now it won't let go of Tom. I've been trying to distract myself all day, but nothing is working. I step forward to put my ragged copy of *Jane Eyre* on the nightstand and almost kick over the two beer bottles on the floor that I drank as I was reading. For a second, the liquor cabinet swims into my mind. Something a little harder than beer might take my mind off of him. I roll a shoulder, somehow dissatisfied with the idea.

I'll go take a walk. That's what I'll do. I throw my book down on the bed and take my staircase two at a time. My mom still isn't home—she's working a double shift and won't be home until early morning. I step onto the well-worn path that leads toward the back of the property and head that way, toward the river and the woods. The smell of the leaves, warmed in summer air, washes over me and lingers in my hair. The little creek that follows the banks in the woods behind my house trickles and traipses over rock and I know when winter comes it will flood its banks with water. I kneel down in the brush, trailing my hand through the cool water, and that's when I hear it. A little cry, like a baby left alone. I wait patiently and sure enough, it comes again. I follow the sound to a patch of tall grass and curled up beneath the stalks is a tiny, smoke-gray kitten. There is no sign of its mother anywhere, and since it's alone, it was probably abandoned. Its eyes are barely open and it's too weak to fight me much when I scoop it up and cup it to my chest. It mews in my arms, scratching me with tiny claws, and I hurry home, already wondering if we have milk in the fridge.

The kitten is so weak that I have to use an eyedropper to feed him. I've determined from the Internet and common sense that the kitten is a boy. He takes nearly three eyedroppers and is too exhausted to take any more and I move him from the kitchen to my room.

"I know I'm not your mother," I say, "but I have a warm blanket for you, and a soft pillow." He curls up on my quilt, an impossibly tiny ball of fur, and instantly falls asleep. I stroke him with a finger as I watch the sun go down. He isn't the first animal I've nursed back to health. There was a cat with a lacerated shoulder and a bird that I coerced into letting me help it for a few days before flying off with his wing not yet healed. I've learned more by doctoring animals than I ever did in school. I wasn't there enough to take much in, and what I did gather I didn't appreciate. I couldn't stand a lot of things about high school, but one of them was definitely the fact that I felt like the teachers spent more time trying to control us than they did teaching us. I would have learned about any subject happily, easily, if they had even bothered to try and understand me instead of treating me like a petulant child. A flash of headlights interrupts my musings and I lean out my window, trying to see who it is. Maybe my mom got off early. The heat rushes suddenly to my cheeks and I half leap off the bed, away from the window as the driver gets out of the car. The headlights shut off and even before my eyes adjust to the darkness I know it's him.

CHAPTER 18
tom

I can see her watching from her window, like Juliet on her balcony. I wait by the car for another second, leaning against the closed door. The air is humid and heavy, adding another layer to my uneasiness. I'm on edge and tense and I have been since I drove away from Alice today. But I couldn't get seeing her out of my mind. I tried to distract myself, thinking after a few hours the need for her would go away. But it didn't. It got worse, and now here I am, standing in front of her house wondering what the hell I'm doing but unable to stop myself.

After what happened on the staircase today I backed off, thinking we could stop then and it would be like it never happened. I could go on pretending I'm not attracted to her and she could go on working at the museum with me and just be my employee. But now it'll never be that way again. Since I've met Alice, since she came to my house and demanded I give her that job, I've been drawn to her. Now I can't even be in her presence without thinking of how she melted under me, how soft her lips are, the way the pulse in her throat was racing. And afterward, she just stared at me, her eyes like liquid gold pouring into me, her lips just a little swollen. I could hear the grandfather clock ticking in the background as the sun came in through the window, lighting up her face.

I'm not like this with girls. I've dated girls, had a couple girlfriends since my freshman year, but none of them were like this. None of them felt like a freight train hurtling down a track at a hundred miles an hour. And I can't get off. Truth be told, I wouldn't get off even if the option were still there. I walk toward the front door with a confidence born of desperation. I can't take another minute of being away from her, even knowing that if I stayed away the possibility of things going back to normal would be a lot more likely. Why would I want things to go back to normal, really? The more I think about life before I met Alice, the less I want to go back.

The front door opens an inch at a time and she's standing in front of me in a flannel shirt that falls past her wrists. Her hair is pulled away from her face. She tucks a strand behind her ear as I watch, her eyes luminous in the dark.

"Hi, stranger," she says, and her voice is the trigger to everything that's been bottled up inside me all day.

"Hi," I say, taking a step toward her. "Is this a bad time?"

"Not at all. You can come in if you want."

I take another step. Neither of us make it inside, because as soon as I'm within six inches of her, she's in my arms. I'm not sure who came to whom but it doesn't matter at this point. The desperation I've felt all day returns with a vengeance. My hands run from her shoulders down her arms to her lower back, slipping under the warmth of her shirt to stroke her skin with my thumbs. Her mouth is soft but fierce as she nips my lower lip and then strokes it with her tongue. I kiss her neck and inhale the scent of coconut and I think I'm going to explode. I pull back, my head reeling. Alice leans into me, tucking her head underneath my chin. She wraps her arms around my waist slowly, like she knows I'm about to fly into a thousand pieces.

"Do you want to come inside?" she says. "For real this time—I won't ambush you again. At least not in the next thirty seconds. There's something I want to show you."

"Okay," I say, and she leads me inside. The house pulls at me, the way it has since the night I carried Alice inside. It's starting to feel more and more comfortable. The first night I walked into tables and knocked Alice's head against the wall carrying her up the stairs, and now I know to avoid that area to the right on the first step because it squeaks.

I haven't been in Alice's room since the night I slept on her floor. It still smells like coconut and incense, but I spot a ball of gray on the bed that wasn't there last time. It uncurls and hisses. Holy shit.

"It's a kitten," I say dubiously, and Alice laughs. She walks over, soothing the kitten that is still fluffed into an angry ball at my presence.

"You act like you've never seen one before," she says.

"I've never seen one that tiny."

"Do you want to hold him?"

"Not particularly," I answer as he spits at me again. Alice just shrugs and cuddles him to her chest. He sits contentedly enough under her chin, still eyeing me suspiciously.

"I found him in the woods today," she says. "I think his mom abandoned him."

"Is that a habit of yours? Finding orphaned animals in the woods?"

She snorts, setting the ball of fur down on the bed.

"No. I've never found a kitten before. But there

are a lot of animals in my woods; I've found other hurts ones and tried to help."

"You're like a modern-day Cinderella," I say dryly, and she laughs. "If fairy tales were real."

"Aren't they?"

"Well, no. They're fiction."

"I'll still take a fairy tale over reality TV. If that's what the world is supposed to be like, I want no part of it."

Sometimes she says things like that, between her bites of sarcasm, something so true it rings through me. I notice the copy of *Jane Eyre* on her nightstand. It's tattered and worn like she's thumbed through it a thousand times.

"*Jane Eyre?*" I ask, holding it up, and she immediately takes it from my hand.

"It's my favorite," she says. She twists it upside down over and over, her head tilted the way a lioness studies her prey.

"It's a good one," I nod, my throat suddenly tight. She sets it down and walks toward me with slow steps. The tension builds again, out of nowhere. The air thickens and my blood turns to fire.

"I think so, too," she says quietly, and I have no idea how she can make those words so erotic. I just stand there, completely drawn to her, until she's only inches away.

"Don't move," she whispers, and I'm a statue. She trails her fingers up the backs of my arms, inch by inch, while her mouth hesitates a fraction of an inch over mine. She slides her hands up the back of my shirt and my entire body reacts to her hands on my skin. Her mouth glides closer to mine; she's close enough to touch, but she told me to be still. My hands are clenched in an effort not to touch her. It's strange to let someone else be in control. Then her mouth is pressed to mine again and all thoughts of control evaporate as I tangle my hands in her hair. The force of it pushes us backward and we stumble together for a few steps until her back hits the wall with a dull thud.

"Sorry," I mutter, but she is already shaking her head and jumping to wrap her legs around my waist.

She kisses me like she may never get another chance, with her entire heart in it, and it's too much for me to process. I've never felt such a complete purity of emotion before, and like everything else about Alice, it attracts and scares me. I've never needed something the way I'm starting to crave her touch, just her presence.

I stumble toward the bed, hoping I'm in the right direction as we both fall, her landing beneath me. Her legs release my waist and I scoot both of us up higher on the bed, so her head is cradled by pillows. We are an impossible tangle of hair and hands and legs and clothes. The kitten has already moved to a more peaceful spot on the floor rug.

Alice is all heat and fire, soft skin and softer curves. Her shirt rides up as my body presses to hers and the skin of her stomach is impossibly smooth. I want to touch her everywhere, taste her everywhere.

"Hold on," says Alice, and her voice is husky. She tugs off her flannel and tosses it on the floor so she's wearing just a tank top. I lean forward and kiss her newly bared skin, starting with the creamy space just beneath her jawline. She shudders beneath me, winding her hands in my shirt, as I kiss my way down her neck an inch at a time. I cup her breasts in my hands, unable to stop myself, wishing our clothes weren't in the way while simultaneously being grateful that they are. I need something to stop me, something to hold me back. I pull back, my hands framing her face as I lie above her on my elbows. She pushes gently on my chest. We roll over on her bed, sending pillows to the floor, until she sits straddled above me, her hands braced on my chest. My thumbs trace circles on her wrists as she leans down, her breasts just brushing my chest. I'm so hard it's painful, and from where Alice is sitting, I know it's obvious. She doesn't seem to care, so I try not to worry about it, but I shift uncomfortably as her body presses down on mine.

"Sorry," she whispers, and I shake my head.

"You're fine," I say, trying not to gasp. She takes my face in her hands and kisses me long and slow. The moment is drawn out like dripping maple syrup—sweet and steady. My hands are on her hips, kneading softly, and then flowing up, under her tank top. She moans softly into my mouth as my fingers swirl over the fabric of her bra. Alice wraps her hands in my hair so tightly that it's on the borderline of painful, but I barely notice. I want to feel her skin; my fingers slide under the fabric. Her breasts fill my hands, her skin so richly soft that all I can think about is my mouth on her. I pull her down, down, until my mouth finds her breast and her breath exhales in a slow gasp of pleasure.

"Oh," she says, grinding her hips against mine. One of my hands is still tangled in her shirt, pulling it down, and my tongue flicks over a bare peak until Alice shudders above me. She threads her fingers with mine and pulls my hands above my head, her clothing settling back over her again. Her eyes connect with mine. They are a dark gold flecked with hazel brown, darker than I've ever seen them. She reaches for the hem of my shirt and tugs it over my head as I lean forward to help her, and then I reach for her shirt in turn. There is a moment of hesitation, as brief as a wing beat, and then she raises her arms so I can tug her tank top off. She reaches around and unhooks her bra herself and I've never seen anything more beautiful than Alice in her own skin. I sit up so we are nose to nose, her positioned in my lap and her legs around my waist. My mouth curves over hers, retreating again and again until she wraps her arms around my shoulders and draws me closer. And finally we're skin against skin, her entire upper body sliding against mine, and I feel as though I've been waiting for this moment forever. I pull back, looking into her eyes. We're both breathing hard, both undone. Her face, inches from mine, is perfect. Her cheeks are flushed pink, her eyes wide and honest. Her hair has come loose and hangs in waves down her back. I want to keep going more than anything in the world, but a part of me holds back. It would be better to wait, safer to wait, than to jump into anything crazy. Of course, Alice's tongue in my ear says otherwise.

"Hold on," I say. "Just hold on."

"Why?"

"Because. Dammit, Alice. Get your tongue out of my ear."

She obliges, but I see her rolling her eyes. I try to focus on something besides the fact that she still doesn't have any sort of top on.

"Why are we stopping? Are you okay?"

Why *are* we stopping? I ask myself. Alice has so much of an effect on me that everything else disappears when I'm with her. I need to pull myself back in.

"Yeah, I'm fine," I say gently. "Are you okay?"

She nods, leaning her head on my shoulder. We rest that way for a few moments, and I'm surprised at how comfortable the quiet is. Alice finally reaches for her flannel and pulls it on, leaving the buttons undone. I can't process how sexy she looks in that shirt, her silky skin peeking through. She stands up and scoops up the kitten from his place on the rug.

"I need to feed him again," she says. "You can help if you want."

I help her feed the kitten, who seems to be marginally more accepting of me now that I've been here a while. Watching her with the eyedropper fascinates me. She feeds the kitten with endless patience, even though I've watched her be unable to sit quietly in a chair for more than three minutes at a time. We head back up to her room, the kitten already falling asleep in her hands.

"Why are so many rooms locked up?" I ask. Alice shrugs.

"They've been that way for a long time," she says. "When I was little, everything was open."

"What happened?"

"He left."

"Who?" I ask as we step into her room.

"My dad," she says, without a trace of rancor. She's just stating a fact, like the color of the sky. I didn't realize it was just Alice and her mom in this big house, but I realize I've never heard her mention a father.

"I'm sorry," I mutter. I never know what to say in these situations.

"Don't be," says Alice. Her chin is in the air, her eyes glittering. "It was a long time ago."

"Do you remember anything about him?"

She sets the kitten down on her bed, and he curls up with a yawn.

"He had eyes like mine. But now I can't remember if I knew that myself or if my mom reminded me about it so many times that I created a memory that was never there."

I nod. I know what it's like to remember the way you loved someone, only to feel it slip farther away each day as your memory fades.

"What about you?" she asks, and my stomach is an instant mass of knots.

"What about me?" I ask, grabbing my shirt and tugging it back over my head.

"Did you know your mom?"

I stare out the window into the night and guess I can't avoid answering the question forever.

"Yeah, I knew her," I say. "She, uh, she passed away a while ago."

"Oh, Tom," says Alice, and her voice physically hurts me. My mom has been gone a long time; it shouldn't hurt anymore. The fact that it does is like another slap in the face by fate.

"Yeah," I say. I hope she doesn't ask me how it happened. I'm not ready to go into that yet. She pulls me down to sit on the edge of the bed next to her and as she shifts toward me I hear the clink of bottles.

"Shit," says Alice. "I meant to throw these away earlier." She lifts two beer bottles from where they've been hidden on the floor next to her bed and my blood runs cold. She sets them both on her night-stand and turns to me like nothing is wrong.

"Why are those there?" I ask.

"I had a couple of drinks earlier, when I was reading."

She blinks at me, her ocher eyes calm and direct. I wrestle with my dual trains of thought. One is reminding me that Alice can do whatever she wants—I'm not in charge of her. My other train of thought wins.

"Seriously?" I say, and Alice's brow furrows.

"Seriously, what?"

"Remember when I picked you up at the party, and you were too drunk to tell me your name?"

"No, actually," she says wryly, and I stand up off the bed.

"I'm not kidding around, Alice."

"What is the big deal? You're mad because I had a couple of beers?"

"I'm the one who picked you up when you were too drunk to stand by yourself. I held your hair when you threw up everything in your stomach."

"What's your point, Tom? That wasn't what happened today."

"Because I've seen what you can be like when you drink," I snap, and her eyes widen.

Sometime in the past minute she's risen from the bed and stands facing me, her arms crossed.

"If I'd known you'd hold it against me, I might have re-thought asking you to pick me up."

"You were too drunk to rethink anything."

"Seriously, Tom, you can't tell me what to do. You're not my parent. Or my boyfriend, for that matter."

Her voice is rising like the wind during a storm, and I know I've tripped one of her wires but I'm too angry to back down.

"Look at your mom," I say, and Alice's nails bite into the skin of her arm. I know I don't know much about her mom, but from the little Alice has told me so far she doesn't sound like the greatest of role models.

"What about her?" She asks the question through gritted teeth.

"Is that what you want to end up like?"

"Don't go there, Tom. Just don't. You know nothing about it."

Her glare is dangerous and her stance widens as she prepares for a fight. Even in the haze of my own anger I'm impressed. Alice doesn't back down from anything.

"I just know you're better than that," I say, and she blinks twice, slowly. "I'm only saying this because I've seen you out of control."

"I didn't ask you to worry about me," she says. "I didn't ask you for anything. And I don't need anything from you, especially your fucking angel attitude. Here's a news flash for you, Tom. If you're looking for someone willing to toe the line, you've got the wrong girl."

"Alice—"

She is already striding out the door. I can hear her rapid footsteps pounding the hallway and I shove my hands into my pockets, standing alone in her room.

CHAPTER 19
tom

I drive home because it's obvious that she wants me to leave. My hands clench on the wheel the entire way home. How did the last part of the night end up so differently from the first? Because if I let myself, I can still feel the shape of her lips against mine, hear the sigh of her breath. I can smell her all over me; she's branded me in more ways than I can name. I lost it when I saw the bottles. If she were anyone else, maybe it wouldn't matter so much, but it's Alice. I've seen her senselessly drunk, and I have more than enough reason in my past to hate alcohol itself with a passion. I can't tell Alice what to do, but that won't stop me from worrying when I see her doing something I know could kill her. That might be dramatic, and I might have overstepped a boundary, but I can still see her on the bathroom floor before I knew if she was breathing.

I shake my head as I put the car into park and open the door. The night air is cool and I breathe in deeply before walking to the apartment and opening the door as quietly as I can. I am desperately uncomfortable with the way Alice and I left things, but tonight I don't think it can be fixed. I need to sleep on it, and so does she. My room seems bleak and dark without her there to brighten it. All I'm surrounded by are shadows and the sound of my own breath. I flick on my reading light and grab the mystery novel I tossed aside earlier, but the words just blur on the page. Will I ever be able to focus on anything besides Alice Bailey ever again?

I lie down on my bed and lock my hands under my pillow, hoping some sleep will clear my head. I close my eyes and the first thing I think of is the flare of her hip, and the soft rise of her breasts where her skin is like butter. I push the thoughts away, striving for a blankness that will lull me to sleep. Even as I settle into the blankets, I sigh, knowing it will take a lot more than that to drive her from my mind.

CHAPTER 20
alice

The sun on my face and the claws of the kitten wake me up, and when I open my eyes I'm surprised to find myself alone before I remember how Tom left. I stretch my arms along my bed, finding nothing but empty sheets. I ran straight to one of the guest rooms last night; it was the first place I could think to go where I could be alone and think clearly. I picked the one with blue walls and white lace comforter because it always calms me down. I was still pacing, hiding there in that room and fuming, when I heard Tom's car leave. I think I was both glad and disappointed to hear him go.

Thinking about last night just pisses me off all

over again. More than anything, I hate being told what to do. It infuriates me so much that it completely overrides what little reason I have in me. I grab a pillow and cover my face with it, breathing in the smell of clean cotton. The kitten mews, biting my feet under the covers with his tiny, sharp, teeth.

"Alright, alright," I say from under the pillow. "Let's feed you." I'm glad I remembered to set up the litter box by my bed. We had a cat a long time ago and the litter box was still in the garage, of course, because we never get rid of anything. I can't even begin to think about the attic. It's packed to the ceiling with boxes and even more furniture. My baby stuff is up there somewhere, hidden in the darkest corner, where my mom hid my dad's boxes. I remember how she put the last lid on the last box and sat there for twenty minutes just staring at the brown cardboard. I don't know why she bothered to keep anything of his. I would have given it away, or better, burned it all piece by piece. I shake the memories away and start feeding the kitten an eyedropper at a time. He's already getting stronger and tomorrow he might be able to start drinking from a bowl on his own. Tom looked at him the same way a man looks at a baby if he's never held one before—with a combination of terror and suspicion.

Tom. What happened last night? The fact that we argued bothers me more than it should; a good fight has never bothered me. But this one does. It's sitting heavy on me and I'm not sure why.

Is it because he might have been a little bit right?

He was controlling and self-righteous. But when I push away the annoyance that his attitude brought on, what he was trying to say might have been a little true. I slap the counter with my hand, turning in a circle. Dammit. I hate being wrong, even a little. Once my temper flares it's impossible for me to calm down. I go over what he said in my head again, over and over—it's stored there, on instant replay. Maybe he annoyed me, and maybe the way he went about it wasn't the best choice, but I think it means that he cares about me. And if that's true, then I owe him an apology. I'm not very good at having someone care enough about me to get mad at me. I'm not used to it.

I finish feeding the kitten and check the time. It's already seven forty-five. If I'm going to get to the museum on time I need to get ready. I start gnawing on my thumbnail. What will seeing him be like? Will it be quiet and awkward? Will he try and avoid my gaze? I shrug to myself. I'm good with fights, but not so good with fixing things. Why'd he have to pick a fight with me, anyway? He should have known it wouldn't end well for him. I smirk to myself and then I head upstairs again, two at a time, so I can jump in the shower before work.

I walk into Tom's office barely five minutes late, swinging around the door and into the room a little breathlessly since I sprinted from my car. Dammit, why can I never be on time?

"Hi," I say, unwinding my mom's scarf from around my neck. It's lavender, with orchids printed on it. If I keep losing her clothes she's going to be mad. "Look, I want to apolo—"

Before I can finish, Tom is out of his seat, crushing me to his chest, his mouth possessive and his hands rough. I don't even have a second to process what's going on. There's no time to calculate, there's only time for my body to respond without a single thought. His lips open mine and his tongue slides inside my mouth as his hands come up to grip my hips so hard I know there will be bruises. But I don't care, my hands are already wound around his neck, and I dimly feel the wall bump into my spine as he pushes me against it. Everything I was going to say trickles out of my mind, replaced by him.

A chair topples over and I hear Tom's door click shut. His mouth begins to race down my neck and he flicks open the first few buttons of my shirt, white silk with pearl buttons. Tom kisses just inside the lace of my bra and I shiver. Feeling his lips there makes every nerve ending in my body sing. Tom's mouth moves, his tongue dipping inside the cup of my bra to tease a nipple. I bite my lip in an effort to stay quiet, my nails digging into his back. I'm very conscious of the fact that we're in his office and anyone could walk in at any moment, but it doesn't make me want to stop. It adds a layer of excitement and thrill that I can't deny. Tom's lips caress my collarbone, then the place where my neck meets my shoulder. My head is tilted back against the wall as I absorb every little thrill his touch sends running down my spine. I already know he's going to stop before he steps away from me, and I don't want him to. I want him to keep going until we're both satisfied, until this wild ache burning low in my belly is gone.

I open my eyes and wait for my vision to clear. Tom is standing in front of me, his body pressed to mine, his hands on the wall on either side of my head. His eyes are dark and intense, pinning me in my place. Tom leans forward, tilting his forehead against mine, and I wait for our heartbeats to slow, hating the space between us. I don't know what's happening to me. Some scale has tipped and now the moments we spend apart grate on my nerves. I run a hand through the hair I just blow-dried and Tom frames my face in his hands. His thumbs stroke my temples and his eyes search my face as though he's never seen anything like me before. I loop my hands loosely around his wrists, leaning into his touch. My head is spinning and my entire body feels like liquid. If he weren't holding me up I'd probably slide into a puddle at his feet.

"You're late," says Tom. His voice is deep and low and something about it makes me shiver.

"I had to shower," I say. "Sorry. I tried to hurry."

"It's okay. Look, about last night—"

"It's fine. You don't have to apologize." I smile into his serious eyes.

"I want to," he says. "I shouldn't have tried to tell you what to do. Or make you feel like a bad person." He pulls away from me and stands with his hands in his pockets.

"I know," I say. "I didn't handle things perfectly either."

A smile quirks up the corner of his mouth. "Is that an apology I'm hearing?"

"Don't push your luck."

"You always surprise me," he says in a low voice.

"I surprise myself too," I say, and he grins.

"I want you to know, I don't see you in a bad way at all," he says. "I just see you the way you were that night and I don't want to see you that way again. You deserve better than that."

I gnaw on my bottom lip as he studies me. It shocks a part of me that he sees me this way, like something precious.

"Thank you," I say. "For that night, again—and for seeing me that way."

"I can't help it," he says, tilting his head. "But you're welcome."

We study each other in the quiet, feeling the shift between us. The air that was thick with tension floods with warmth.

"There were other parts," I say, "about last night that weren't so bad."

"Weren't so bad?" parrots Tom. He grins.

"Yeah," I say, shrugging. "They were okay."

"I think they were more than okay," he says, stepping toward me. I tilt my head up so my lips are inches from his, teasing him.

"But you stopped us," I say.

Tom nods, looking uncomfortable.

"It was a little intense. I felt like I needed to back off for a minute."

"Yeah. It was intense for me too. Has it been that way for you before? With other girls?"

As soon as I ask, I see the way his face changes. It closes off even more than usual, and his eyes break away from mine. *Oh*, I think. *Oh*. Well then.

"Are you a virgin?" I ask quietly, and his eyes snap up to meet mine. He walks back to his desk and sits down, folding his arms on the table.

"Yeah," he says, and a flush of color creeps up his neck.

"Oh," I say, plopping down in my chair in front of him. "Well, that's not a big deal."

"How many eighteen-year-old guys do you know who are virgins?"

I roll my eyes. What a male response.

"You know, I don't have the statistics off the top of my head. It's not a bad thing, Tom."

He shrugs, still looking uncomfortable.

"I take it you're not, then," he says, glancing up at me.

"Nope."

He looks like he wants to know more, but doesn't ask, and I don't say. I can't always be the one volunteering information. Sooner or later he has to learn to communicate what he's feeling.

"You don't care?" he asks softly, and I take his hand on the desk.

"Why would I care?" I say. "It doesn't matter to me at all, either way."

He still looks uncomfortable. Something I'm starting to realize about Tom is that a part of him is shut off from the rest of the world. He opens up to me with bits and pieces of information at a time, like a door letting in sunlight. And that's fine with me for the most part. But I feel so transparent to him that sometimes I wish he wouldn't close himself off to me so much.

"Well, let's get started with today's agenda," he says, and I settle back in my chair to take my orders.

The rest of the day passes quickly. Tom keeps me busy with marketing stuff and takes me on a tour of the next floor of the museum. I'm becoming more familiar with the layout and with some of the other employees at the museum. Security knows me well, since they let me in everyday, and everyone else is still being introduced to me person by person. People are generally busy in their offices, but a few have poked their heads into Tom's office to talk to him about something and he always introduces me. Most of the time though, it's just us.

I like listening to Tom talk about the museum. I never hear him talk as much as he does when he's telling me some new fact. I wonder again what his connection is to it—it feels more intense than just a job that came out of volunteer work. Not only does he seem to know more about history than anyone I've ever met, he talks about the museum as though he's a part of it. He knows every detail there is to know about the place, from the floor plans to something as mundane as what the every-day hours are. Even when he goes off on some new tangent about it, he never bores me. I am more drawn to him when he reveals bits and pieces of his passion.

I'm sitting in my chair next to Tom's desk working on a marketing proposal when the air changes. It thickens with something like humidity that washes over my skin and makes my spine crackle. I glance up and Tom is staring at me with an intensity that turns my knees to jelly. I press my thighs together, trying to temper the ache. My body is already so tuned to him that one look turns me into a shivering pool of nerves. I glance down at my watch and start to gather my stuff together to leave. He just sits, perched in his chair like a sexy, green-eyed CEO, with his fingers linked together and his elbows resting on his desk. He watches me gather my papers and my bag and I hope he doesn't notice the way my hands are trembling. His eyes on me are making me crazy. Finally, I straighten up and arch an eyebrow in his direction.

"Is it alright by you if I head out now, sir?" I ask pertly, and his lips curve up into a smile.

"Yeah, you can go," he says quietly. I bite my lower lip, my eyes flicking over him, and I watch his gaze go dark and his knuckles flex. I smirk at him and spin around, striding out of the room before either of us can come to the other. Our first day working together since things changed is over and I'm glad. I don't think I could have sat quietly in the same room with him another hour. I walk out the front door of the museum and gulp in the hot summer air. It's not exactly refreshing, but it's not staring at me from across the room and making me slowly lose my mind.

The week seems to pass both achingly slow and mind-blowingly fast, like a roller coaster ride that winds through the days. It's getting harder and harder for Tom and I to stay away from each other during the day. More than once this week we've ended up in one of the museum's empty rooms or behind exhibits desperately grabbing at each other only to spring apart as someone walks by. Luckily, the museum has been closed for repairs to everyone but staff for the past two weeks, so no guests stumbled across Tom with his hands in my shirt behind the Civil War display. I get to my car at the end of the day on Friday and sit down, laying my head on the steering wheel. My nerves are raw from the ups and downs of being with Tom and being away from him. Neither of us has brought up seeing each other outside of work since the beginning of the week. I think of the lonely weekend ahead of me and sigh. I guess I should head home.

For the first time in my life, my big house feels empty as I walk inside. My mom is asleep and heading to a night shift so it's just going to be Napoleon and me. Since he's so tiny and feisty, that's what I've named the kitten. I told Tom and he laughed out loud. I head up to my room and say hi to Napoleon before I change for a shower, trying to push thoughts of Tom from my mind. I wonder if he's thinking of me. I wonder if he takes long showers like I do and in the same moment I know he doesn't. He would take short, efficient showers, military-style. He and I are different in that way. We're different in a lot of ways. Sara texts me asking if I want to go out, but for the first time the thought of spending the night drunk somewhere holds little appeal for me. The night ends with me cuddled up with Napoleon, falling asleep early to the sound of a summer breeze outside my window.

CHAPTER 21
alice

Something wakes me late at night, and I lay still for a breathless moment in the dark. All I can hear is the beating of my heart in my ears and the whoosh of my shallow breaths. Then it comes again: a shuffle in the dark, followed by the click of my door. My teeth are clenched I'm so terrified, but I tense up and prepare to spring. If someone is here to kill me or rob me they're not going to do it without a fight. Another shuffle—this time closer. Something slithers along the foot of my bed and I lunge toward it, opening my mouth to scream.

A hand claps itself over my mouth. A familiar

weight pins me to the bed even as I flail, and I hear the hiss as one of my blows lands.

"Alice! Alice, calm down. It's me."

"What the hell?"

"It's Tom. I'm sorry—I wasn't sure if your mom was here and I didn't want to wake her up."

"Why didn't you just call me?"

"I did. You didn't answer."

"Oh. Well, yeah, I was sleeping."

"I noticed."

My eyes start to adjust, and the light from the moon that comes in through my window is enough for me to see his face. He is smiling at me. I grin back, half out of pure delight at seeing him and half at the ludicrous situation. I clap a hand over my own mouth and start giggling and Tom starts laughing too. He has the best laugh to listen to— warm and low. I lift my hand to his cheek out of pure affection and he kisses my palm.

"You came," I whisper, and he nods.

"I'm here," he says, taking my hand to trace circles on it. He's on the edge of my bed and I'm sitting up against my pillows, our faces bare inches apart. His hand stills on mine. My breathing slows, my cheeks flush. I slide closer, scrunching the quilt between us. Tom pulls it aside and his arm slides around my lower back and pulls me to him. I'm unprepared. I've just woken up and I had no idea he'd be here. But there's no hesitation in my veins, no will to pull away. The moment stills and lengthens and Tom leans over and finally, finally his lips are on mine and there's all the time in the world for me to learn his body from touch alone. I stand up and I can see myself illuminated in the light of the moon. His eyes are dark, focused on me, and I take the tank top I wore to bed and sweep it off of me in one smooth motion. I slip out of my soft shorts and stand in from of him in nothing but moonlight.

"You're perfect," he says, and I swear my skin glows. I step toward him and he reaches for me, pulling me onto the bed. I roll onto my back and Tom links his fingers with mine and pulls my hand above my head. My pulse is racing and my back arches as every inch of me strains closer to him and finally his mouth starts to flow over my neck. I reach for his shirt, tugging it over his head. His chest is smooth and hard and I run my hands over him again and again, leaning up to kiss the skin over his heart. My fingers move to trace the ridges of his back and shoulders as his tongue skims over the hollow of my throat. My legs twine around his and catch in the fabric of his jeans. The rough material feels intrusive against my bare skin. I move my hands to his hips, tracing the hollows, and then unbutton his jeans. He stills, looking down at me.

"Is this okay?" I ask, and he nods and kisses me, his hands on either side of my face, and then stands briefly to take his jeans off and step out of them before coming back to the bed. He lies next to me and I can't stop touching him. He called me perfect but he's the perfect one. I push him gently onto his back and move toward the end of the bed and take his hardness in my hands. Tom hisses out a breath through clenched teeth, an arm thrown over his brow. I lean down and taste him gently and he sits up on the bed in one rough motion.

"Come here," he commands, his voice husky, and I move back to the pillows. I arch toward him with my hand on his chest, an invitation. My body needs him so badly, to be caressed and taken by his touch. He shifts his body away, turning so we are face to face, with his hands on either side of my head. He moves himself above me again, kissing me gently, and I respond, but I'm a little frustrated with the distance I can feel him placing between us. What does he want? He stands up and grabs his jeans off the floor, pulling a condom out of his pocket.

"Let me," I say, sitting up on the bed. He steps toward me, hands me the foil wrapper and I tear it open and slowly roll it down his length. His eyes burn into me, watching my every movement, but he doesn't touch me, and the confusion pulls my mind out of the moment. I don't have time to dwell on it before he is above me again, leaning on his elbows so his hands frame my face. He kisses me briefly and my lips reach up after his.

"Are you okay?" he asks, and I nod, spreading my hands over his shoulders. He leans over me, his body finally pressed flesh to flesh against mine, and I reach down to guide him inside me.

"Here," I say. "Here, like this."

At the first moment of joining he shudders and stills, his body rigid above mine. His eyes are squeezed shut for three full seconds as I shift beneath him.

"Are you okay?" I ask, stroking his face, and he nods sharply. His eyes open and lock onto mine with an intensity that shoots straight into me. Everything he's feeling and experiencing is broadcast there in light and color. He starts to move, my hands on his hips, letting him discover the rhythm of our bodies. I moan, reaching my lips up toward his, and he kisses me briefly before shifting above me. He speeds up, and tears fill my eyes in reaction to the emotion welling up inside me. Our bodies are beautiful together, and having him inside me is indescribable. It's like a part of me I didn't know was missing has been reconnected. I wrap my legs around his waist and cling to him as he arches and his entire body tenses. He collapses on top of me, his slick skin hot on mine. His chest rises and falls, his heart beating so fast I can feel it better than my own. He shifts his face away from mine and a tear escapes, flowing down my cheek, and I don't know why.

CHAPTER 22
tom

I'd never seen anything as beautiful as Alice standing naked in front of me. There's no part of her that is self-conscious or nervous. I saw the flush in her cheeks and the way she was biting her lip but she didn't hide from me. Her eyes shone almost gold in the moonlight, and the glow of them won't leave my mind. I tossed and turned for hours before I finally got up the courage to come to her. I laid there with my hands locked under my head and the sheet in a pile at the foot of my bed and I couldn't get her out of my mind. This week has been overwhelming in a way that I can't even begin to explain. She's like a drug that I can't stop taking but the side effects are messing with my head. Everything with her is a first—and that's nothing if not dangerous.

I lay there with her afterwards, too lost in the afterglow to even consider forming words. I never knew. I never knew it could be anything like that. No girl I've ever dated, or known, for that matter, compares to Alice. She gives me so much of herself, nothing held back. I have a hard time doing the same. Even as I lay on top of her, her fingers tracing patterns on my back, it's almost painful to be so close to her. When she was touching me, when she had her mouth on me . . . it was so intense I couldn't stand it. I wanted to spend eternity touching her, learning every curve of her body, but I know I rushed it. No one ever told me that, either—that you could love someone so much that it bordered on pain. As soon as the thought rolls through my mind, I remove the word *love* from the sentence. I like her. A lot. She fascinates me, entertains me. I could spend all day with her and never be bored.

She shifts beneath me and looks up, smiling

softly, and something twists inside me, two forces at war: I'm in love with her. I'm not in love with her.

"You okay up there?" she asks, and I let myself have a moment lost in her voice.

"Yeah, yeah. I'm fine."

"It's different the first time," she murmurs, stroking my face.

"Yeah," I say, swallowing hard. It was intense. More intense than she could possibly know. "I know it wasn't perfect, but—"

She puts a hand over my mouth.

"Don't say that," she says. "It was wonderful. You don't need to apologize or feel like you should have done something different."

In my chest there's a physical aching. I try to pull it in, to get a handle on my emotions. I shift so I'm lying next to her instead of on top of her, and she snuggles up to me and lays her head on my shoulder. Her head is tucked perfectly under my chin, as though she belongs exactly there. Within sixty seconds, I feel her breathing slow. She falls asleep like a child, instantly and in any situation. I pull her closer to me and she sighs in her sleep, burrowing her nose into my neck. Her hair is a golden waterfall on the pillow, shimmering in the pieces of moonlight that make it through the window. Everything about this picture is so beautifully simple. But in reality, it's much more complicated. I don't know how to go about loving Alice. Everything I feel when I'm with her is so blindingly powerful that it's almost physically painful. Love shouldn't hurt, right? I shake my head. What do I know? What the hell do I know about any of this?

Gently, trying not to wake her, I disentangle myself from Alice. She mumbles a little in her sleep but readily takes the pillows I tuck into her arms as my replacement. As I pull my clothes back on I find a furry ball sleeping on my pants—the kitten must have jumped down off the bed when I got here. What did she say she'd named him? Napoleon. I grin as I set him back down on the bed, where he curls promptly into a ball at the foot of the quilt. I kiss Alice's cheek, amazed at the softness of her skin, and brush her hair back from her face. She's still in the moonlight except for the rise and fall of her breaths, her hair a spill of gold. I leave silently, closing the door behind me, wondering what the hell I've gotten myself into. There is a tightness in my chest, and an urgent desire both to go right back to her and to get away someplace where I can attempt to think clearly. When I'm with Alice, she fills my entire mind, leaving no room for reason. I head home slowly, taking care in the dark, picturing Alice safe and asleep in her big house in the woods.

I text Alice as soon as I get home, telling her there was something I was needed for and that I had to go. It's bullshit—who could need me at two in the morning?—and I don't know if she'll believe it. But I couldn't stay. If I stayed I would have watched her wake up in my arms and told her I loved her instantly. And that can't happen. It hurts too much to be right. It can't be right. And so I end up right back where I started, lying on my back in my bed and thinking of Alice. I wish there was some black and white line that would tell me what was right, which side to be on. My instincts and my mind are at war with each other. Moonlight shimmers through the gap in my curtains and I picture it falling over Alice's face. I wish I were there to see it. Eventually I fall into a restless sleep, waking up throughout the night in fits and starts, dreaming of her.

The rest of the weekend passes achingly slowly. Alice responds to my text saying no problem and she hopes I worked out whatever the problem was with my dad. I make up an excuse as to why I can't see her again until Monday and go back to brooding. Almost every part of me wants to go over there and take her in my arms and never let her go, but there's a tiny part of me that's protesting. What makes the most sense here is getting my feelings for her under control. I say it to myself again in my head as though if I repeat it enough times it will become the truth. I get ready for bed on Sunday night with a mixture of excitement and trepidation. I get to see her tomorrow. I've missed her since I saw her last. I go to bed early, but my mind won't turn off. I lay there for hours and hours, trying to get comfortable. I can't get her out of my mind. Every time I begin to doze off, I start to dream of the winding corridor that leads to her room or the brightness of her smile, and I jolt awake again. A part of me hopes that she's holding a pillow in that big house and pretending that it's me. I finally doze off around two in the morning, dreading and praying for daylight.

CHAPTER 23
tom

Monday introduces itself rudely, as usual, with an annoying buzzing sound coming from my dresser. It's a text from Alice. I open it, rubbing my bleary eyes so I can read it.

Want a ride to work? I've got coffee and bagels. I was up early. The apocalypse is here.

I grin through the film of exhaustion. A ride to work can't hurt, right? I rub a hand over my face and then jump up and head for the shower. I need to hurry to be done before she's here. I can't believe she's early—she's never even on time. I hurry through my shower and get dressed before moving to the living room. I never watch TV in the mornings, but I'm so nervous I just turn it on and flip to a channel without thinking. I've just sat down on the couch when there is a knock on the door. I jump a foot in the air and try to walk slowly to make it look like I wasn't waiting for her to get here, feeling like an idiot. I open the door.

Will she always have this effect on me when I see her? Every single time? She has her hair up, pulled away from her face, and something pink slicked over her lips. She is wearing a long-sleeved dark blue dress, tight, that goes all the way to her knees but still shows every curve. I inhale and catch a heady whiff of her scent and there is an instant jolt as my mind recognizes it as Alice.

"Hi," she says quietly, smiling at me.

"Hi," I answer. "Come in."

She grins and waltzes in as though she's been here to have coffee and bagels with me a thousand times before. I can't stop staring at her. She sets the coffee cups and the bag down on my kitchen table and I come up behind her, slipping my arms around her waist. She leans back into my embrace, turning her head to kiss my cheek. Everything is a little different, again. I can feel it. One night, one night with Alice, and everything is changed. But there's no trace of awkwardness. I don't think Alice knows how to do anything awkwardly.

"I can't believe you snuck out on me again," she teases, pulling a bagel from the bag.

"Uh, yeah," I say. "I'm sorry about that."

"It's okay," she says. "Maybe next time you could actually stay. I promise to share the covers."

"Next time?"

"Yeah."

She stops spreading cream cheese on her bagel and looks up at me, grinning. I want to say yes, of course, there will be another time, but something on the TV catches my eye. A name rings in my head, a name I know.

"Tom?" Alice's voice sounds as though it's coming from underwater. The broadcaster's voice is loud in my ears, so clear it's painful.

"Part of the new Second Chances Program

installed by Mayor Ansley, a Mr. Howie Barker was released from the Richmond Correctional Facility this morning on parole. Mr. Barker was convicted nearly six years ago for vehicular manslaughter while intoxicated. A woman was killed in the accident; her son, also in the vehicle, survived."

No. *No, no, no.* This isn't real. He was supposed to serve at least ten years. He had a prior record, a few felonies. His blood-alcohol content was off the charts. He wasn't supposed to see the light of day for another four years.

"Tom. Tom, you're scaring me. What's going on?"

My entire body has gone cold. My stomach is a pit of cramps. Alice's voice is frightened, but I can't bring myself to comfort her. I grip the side of the couch with one hand so hard I can hear the fabric seams tearing.

"Tom, talk to me. What's wrong?"

I don't know how to say it. The words are stuck in my throat, like all the rest of the important things I can never say. I have to tell her.

I lift my head but cannot meet her eyes. I sit

down on the edge of the couch, and Alice sits next to me, grabbing my hand. There is a moment of silence broken only by the murmur of the TV in the background. Alice's eyes are wide, searching my face. I have to tell her. I can't. I shake my head, helpless.

"Your hand is like ice," she whispers.

"It's nothing," I try to say. The words lodge in my throat like pebbles and Alice's eyes narrow into slits.

"That's him," comes a voice from behind us, and Alice and I both turn to find my father behind us, staring at the TV. He is barefoot and unshaven, and as he stares at the man who killed his wife, his son's mother. He is someone I don't recognize.

"What are you talking about?" asks Alice. "Someone tell me what's happening."

I try to say no, to tell him to stop, but when I open my mouth nothing comes out.

"He's the one," says my father. "Renee and Tom were driving home from school. Howie Barker was driving, too. He was drunk."

I can see it all flashing in front of me—the gray of the asphalt, the red of my mother's hair. Her voice is tense, arguing with me about a math grade, and then I can't hear anything but the screech of metal on metal.

Alice's face is a mask, completely white, her eyes flicking from the TV to me. I am numb. Alice's hand in mine is distant, as though she's touching me through a film. I'm on one side of the glass and she's on the other. This is all a dream. A nightmare. Just like that day.

"Renee was thrown from the car. On the way to the hospital, she went into cardiac arrest as a result of her injuries and her heart stopped. Tom survived." My dad's voice is mechanical, as though he's reading the words from a screen.

"Tom?" Alice whispers. "Tom, say something please."

I can't meet her eyes.

"I can't believe he's out," whispers my dad, and it's too much for me to handle.

"He's not supposed to be allowed parole for at least another four years," I manage.

"It's a new program. Relief from certain sentences

for good behavior. It's supposed to help relieve over-crowded jails."

I shake my head, yanking my hand from Alice's. My dad is a ghost—I see him right in front of my eyes, but it's like he's barely there. He turns and walks back into his office with heavy steps, leaving Alice and me alone. Seconds of silence tick by while I try to control the way my hands are shaking.

"Tom," Alice says in a low voice. "Why didn't you tell me?"

"I couldn't," I mutter. "I don't talk about it."

"You were in the car with her?"

I nod, miserable. I wish I never would have turned the TV on and seen that. I wish I could've gone on thinking that lowlife was still rotting in prison, where he belongs.

"I'm so sorry," she whispers. "I wish you would have told me. You could have told me. I would have understood."

"Oh, really?" I snap at her. "You think so? I don't."

"Okay, there's no reason to get mad at me. I know this must be hard—"

"You don't know shit about this. This happened a long time ago. It shouldn't matter anymore. It doesn't matter anymore."

"You can't keep your feelings bottled up like this."

"They're not bottled up."

"They are!"

Alice is standing up now, her cheeks spots of red. Her fists are clenched.

"This is obviously still killing you, Tom. It might have happened a long time ago but it's not over for you."

I bury my face in my hands. "I don't want to talk about this. It's nothing you need to know about."

"If you think I didn't have a right to know about this, you're wrong," she says with so much vehemence I look up.

"Do you think I can't see the way you hold yourself back from me? You never talk about the way you're feeling, ever. About anything. You barely touched me that night. We made love and you barely touched me."

Her voice catches in her throat and I hate myself.

"You can't live with your emotions hidden in a box inside yourself. It'll eat you alive from the inside out."

"I don't need your advice," I say with my teeth clenched. "The last thing I need, actually, is advice from someone not fucking smart enough to pass high school history."

It's a low blow, a desperate one. Her sympathy is like salt in my still-bleeding wounds. I can't bring myself to let it begin to heal me. To my surprise, Alice laughs. The sound is cold and jarring.

"You really think that is going to hurt me?" she says. "I see right through you. If you won't let me in, fine. But don't expect me to sit here and fucking baby you while you cry about how hard your life is. Wake up and deal with what's in front of you."

Her words sting me with every syllable, but I'm motionless. I've never heard her voice so hard or so cold. I look up and Alice's beautiful eyes are filled with tears. A part of me tears into two pieces as she runs out of the apartment, leaving the coffee and bagels behind. I don't move. I don't go after her. My chest aches, and I let it. I never deserved her anyway.

CHAPTER 24
alice

The last weeks at the museum drag by one day at a time as Tom and I continue to ignore each other. I've never heard a story so tragic. I don't know how Tom thought he could keep it inside. The second day after that terrible morning at the apartment, I walked into his office thinking he'd still be out and there he was. He looked up when I came in as though he had no greater concern than the stack of papers he handed to me. He sat in his chair all day and handed me assignments silently and that was it. I sat within three feet of him and pretended not to notice the tension even when it felt like my chest would shatter into a thousand pieces with the effort of holding back tears. I can't stop thinking about the night we made love. Was it all just a joke to him, a game? Was he using me to try and relieve some of his pain? I just don't know. I saw a side of Tom I've never seen and it's making me second-guess everything.

I want to give him comfort so badly. I sit in his office with my laptop and he sits and types and I want so badly to hold him and tell him that it's okay. Everything he said to me and the way he pushed me away hurts less than knowing how much pain he's in and not being able to help. But that's not my decision. Tom won't let himself be helped right now. He wasn't the only one hurt in this arrangement. If he wants to carry around baggage of his own, fine. But when that baggage starts to affect me, it's not fair anymore.

I'd like to think, even if our relationship wasn't officially defined, that he would care about me enough not to do that to me. The sad part is that Tom has changed me in a way I notice every day. I sit up straighter, I stand a little taller. Somewhere along the line between when he picked me up drunk from that party and made love to me he made me realize I'm worth more than I'd been giving myself. I treat myself a little better because of how he treated me. I try to listen to myself the way he did, completely focused on what mattered to me. I miss that. I miss him.

He hasn't spoken a word to me since that day. Every day, instead of getting easier, it hurts a little more. If he wants to get through the rest of my internship agreement without speaking a word to me, fine. I can play that game just as easily as he can. I can sit and pretend not to care about anything but the keyboard in front of me. He doesn't have to know that I go home every day and let the tears come until I'm cried out and the pillows are soaked.

CHAPTER 25
tom

There's no way to repair the damage I've done to Alice and me. After she left that day, I spent a long time thinking about it and decided it just made more sense for everyone if I stayed away from her. I just kept seeing that look on her face after I yelled at her. Knowing that I made her feel that way hurt more than anything else. I can't risk that happening again. I just let the days at the museum go by, enduring the torture it is to have her sitting so close to me and to see her face looking like stone. Her last few days are finally here and I'm relieved. I don't know how much longer I'd be able to do this.

I'm sitting at my kitchen table, going over a few

items of business from my boss, when my phone starts to buzz. For a painfully hopeful moment, I think I'll see Alice's name on the screen, but when I look it's just Mr. Henry. I rub a hand over my face and answer it. I've been touching base with him on Alice's progress and behavior during her work at the museum. It must be time for another update.

"Hello?"

"Hello, Tom, how are you?"

"Great," I lie.

"I'm just checking in for another update about Alice. The last time we spoke it sounded as though everything was going smoothly."

"Yes, very. It's been great."

"She's been there every day? Are her hours on track?"

"Yes to all of the above." It pleases me, on some small plane, to praise Alice. She deserves every word.

"That's wonderful. She should be finishing up at the end of this week, then?"

"That's right."

There is a familiar twist in my stomach at the

thought of Alice leaving. I'll probably never see her again.

"I have to say, Tom—I'm impressed. I never thought we would be able to get Alice to stick with something like this. You must have made some sort of impression on her."

"Not at all. She's a very caring, dedicated intern, and she's done great work for us."

"You sound as though you know a side of her I don't," the vice principal chuckles.

It's true, I think. *Because you don't know her the way I do.* She isn't the kind of girl you can figure out in an hour or even a day. She holds so much right on the surface, but when you look closer, it's clear that that's all superficial. If you want to know her, really know her, you need to dig deeper. Peel back her layers one by one and you'll start to see who she really is. She's passionate, incredibly smart, impetuous, and intuitive. And I'm an idiot. I'm an idiot who loves her and could have had her, and ruined it.

"You seem to have made an impression on her

right back," Mr. Henry continues. "She said she greatly admires you."

"What?"

"That's what she said. She said you're a good supervisor but your strength lies in your passion about the museum and your integrity. She said she wouldn't have worked for anyone but you. Knowing Alice, that's a true statement."

"When did she say this?"

"I just got off the phone with her before I called you."

"Right. Right, well, thanks a lot, Mr. Henry."

"It's my pleasure. Thank you again for everything, Tom. Alice is one of my favorite students. It's been immensely pleasing to watch her succeed over the past few weeks."

"It's been my pleasure as well. Goodbye, Mr. Henry."

"Goodbye, Tom."

I hang up and my mind is whirling. She said those things about me? It wasn't *I love you, Tom. Please come back to me*, but at least she doesn't hate me. I hold onto that singular thought: *She doesn't hate me.* I stand up and start to pace in the kitchen from the fridge to the table and back. I think about all the things we said to each other and how much it hurt. But she was right. I was closed off to her. She brought out too much emotion in me and that made it hard to keep everything bottled up—including the pain. I couldn't separate all the hate and anger inside myself from the love I felt for her.

She doesn't hate me.

I can't be a coward anymore. It might not do any good but I have to go talk to her. At the very least, I can apologize. She deserves that much. She deserves so much more than that much.

I pull into her driveway with butterflies erupting from my stomach into my throat. I am shaking, both from nervousness and just the anticipation of seeing her again. I walk to the front door and knock and wait, but there's no answer. My phone is in my car and I don't want to go get it so I open the door on my own. The inside of the house is familiar and welcoming, but I don't have time to admire it now.

I have to see her. I fly up the stairs and down the hallway to the room at the back of the house. Her door is halfway open; I nudge it the rest of the way and see her sitting on her bed, Napoleon on her lap. She looks up from *Pride and Prejudice* with a look of surprise, and then her face closes off. I wonder how many times she's seen that look from me. I've never been more scared in my life than I am right now, standing in front of Alice, about to lay my heart at her feet. I don't know if she'll take it. I don't know if I would if I were in her place. I've done so many things wrong. But maybe, just maybe, I can make it all right.

CHAPTER 26

alice

"What are you doing here?" I ask.

Seeing him in this room again hurts. Just the sight of him brought on a new flash of pain in my chest. His eyes are impossibly green in the light coming through my window, and they're so sad it makes my heart ache. I can see his heart shining through his eyes, the way they have before. But I need more than that. I need the words.

"Alice," he says, and his voice is enough to break me. It feels like an eternity since I've heard it. "I'm, uh . . . not very good at stuff like this." He walks into the center of my room. "Let me start by saying that I'm sorry."

My breath chokes in my throat.

"Not just for that day."

He comes a step closer.

"For all of it," he says. "You were right. I was closed off from you because I loved you and I had no concept of how to handle it."

The word *love* shoots through me like a barbed blade. I am speechless for most likely the first time in my life. I draw my knees to my chest on the bed, at a complete loss.

"I had so much pain I was trying to deal with," Tom continues. "Everything I felt for you got in the way."

I remember his ragged breaths, the grip of his fingers.

"I didn't want to love you," he says gently. "But I didn't have that choice. You didn't give me one."

He takes a step closer.

"And if you don't feel the same, that's okay. I wouldn't blame you. I just couldn't let this end without you knowing what you are to me."

There is a strange warmth spreading through my chest to the tips of my toes.

"And I should have told you about my mom," he admits. "It was a burden I didn't think you should have to bear. And it had been mine for so long that I didn't know how to share it with someone else."

"I would never want you to bear something like that alone," I say. "I would have helped you, if you would have let me."

"I know that now," Tom says, running a hand through his already messy hair. "I knew it then, too. I just couldn't."

I nod and just look at him. He stands on my rug, Napoleon at his feet, and just looks at me. Not through me, or around me—right at me. And now I know, without a doubt, that it's because there isn't anything I could say that he would think was stupid or insignificant.

"It will take me some time," says Tom. "I'm not saying I can change this in a day. But I want to work on it. I want to be different. Before you came along, I was living in black and white. I don't want to go back."

His voice is low, honest, and his eyes are pleading. He stands in front of me with his heart in his eyes and I think I'm dreaming, to hear the words coming out of his mouth. It's been hell, living without him, and knowing he was hurting without me being able to help. Having him here now is more than I ever dared to hope for. In that moment, my heart flip flops in my chest and I reach a hand toward him.

Tom lunges toward me at the same time I stand up to meet him and our lips meet hungrily, desperately. He feels so good and I didn't realize how much I missed him until I touched him again. He takes my face in his hands and kisses me deeply, then wraps his arms around my waist. Tendrils of desire snake their way up from my toes, making my entire body tingle.

"You're an ass," I say, and he laughs.

"That's your response to my apology?"

"Yes," I say, pushing away from him. "Because you are. You're unbearably stubborn and opinionated and serious. But you also make me feel alive and wanted, like I matter."

My voice quivers, because it's so true. I can almost feel the words reverberate through my body.

"You do matter," Tom whispers. He leans in and kisses the corner of my mouth, the curve of my cheek, my temple. My heart swells.

"I'm so sorry I couldn't give you what you needed the first time," he says. "Let me try again."

He scoops me up in his arms and I wrap my arms around his neck. He carries me with slow, careful steps to my bed and sets me down gently on my back. On his hands and knees above me, he leans down to kiss me before moving to my shirt.

"I loved it when you did this for me," he says in a low voice, unbuttoning my shirt. "But this time, let me."

All I can do is nod, arching beneath his hands. My body is yearning for him, already needy. He unbuttons my shirt achingly slowly, flicking one button at a time, and then slides it off my arms. My tank top is next, and he leans down to kiss the swell of my breasts above my bra before unhooking it and discarding it on the floor with my shirt.

"You're so unbelievably gorgeous," he says, and he leans forward to kiss his way from the hollow of my hip to my nipple. I gasp, my hands in his hair as his tongue swirls around the peak. This is the lover I knew that he could be—gentle and kind, but passionate. He kisses his way back to my hips where my jeans are buttoned and unhooks them, pulling the zipper down and pulling them off my legs. He moves forward and kisses me through my panties, his warm breath sending thrills down my legs. I twist above him, my hands grabbing handfuls of the quilt.

"I loved when you did this for me last time, too," says Tom. "And I'm sorry I was stupid enough not to give it back."

He slides my panties down my legs and his tongue flicks over me. I moan, my muscles tensing as his mouth explores the tender skin of my inner thighs before finding my sex again. Finally, it's too much to bear. I raise my arms, reaching for him, and he's there instantly. His clothes are off in seconds, his skin finally pressed to mine. We roll on top of the sheets, tangled in each other. His hands flow over every inch of me, and I can't say how good it is to shudder and sigh, surrendering to his touch. He reaches into his pants pocket and grabs another condom, fitting it over himself with hurried fingers.

When he rises over me, I am already reaching for him. He leans down and bites my lower lip gently as he positions himself between my legs. There is so much tenderness, so much care. His eyes search mine, reading my face, and I smile and nod, giving him the signal he was waiting for. I dig my nails into his back, crying out as he slides inside me. I hear him groan and the sound makes my eyes swell with tears. I love knowing that I can do this to him and for him; take him to a place where it's just him and me and the rest of the world fades into the distance. He buries his face into my neck as he moves and I can barely stand the joy of it. My heart spills out of me in invisible silken strands, and I lay it at his feet, with nothing held back. There is a power in that I didn't know, a kind of strength that comes from giving everything you have to give, even knowing the risks. I wrap my legs around his waist and he links his fingers with mine, a connection I hold on to as everything but he and I ceases to exist.

Afterward, I hold him until his breathing slows and I have the pleasure of being the one who watches him fall asleep. I get up and walk to my window, where the sun is still shining. I look down at myself, half expecting to see someone completely different. I let the warmth of the sunshine wash over me, my eyes closed.

"Alice?" Tom's sleepy voice calls from the bed, and I turn and run into his arms, the feeling of sunshine embedded into my skin like a tattoo. I run to him and toward my confidence in myself. I run toward the future that I hope for both of us. And I run toward love, because I deserve it, I want it, and because I know in my heart of hearts that Tom is someone who can give me something that no one else in this world can.

Tom's arms surround me, and everything disappears into blurred edges. There is only us and what we bring to each other, and the brave and bold hope that it's enough to last forever.